Tied Up for Love

For Love Novella Series
Book 1

Nora Lane

First Editor: Cassidy @ Cassidy Hudspeth Edits

Proofreading: Sara @ Simply Write Editing

Interior Design: Elana @ Page & Polished

Cover Design: Nora Lane @noralanewrites

Character Art: Maria Teressa Quinamco, @essasketch

ISBN (paperback): 979-8-9932867-1-6

ISBN (ebook): 979-8-9932867-0-9

 Formatted with Vellum

Blurb

**He's tasked to pull off a kidnapping.
Fate gives him the wrong twin.**

The absolute last thing book-obsessed Charlotte Bennett expects while browsing the bookstore is to be kidnapped by grumpy ex-Marine, Aiden Carter—the man tasked to abduct her twin sister.

Charlotte is forced into his vehicle with bound hands and a sack over her head, her heart tripping with nerves—the good and bad kind—while a scowly broad-shouldered man drives her into a panic.

When an unexpected stop allows Charlotte to get to know the man responsible for her abduction, the chemistry in the air charges with tangible proof of a dark romance gone right.

Suddenly, she starts to wonder if the man who tied her up could also be the one to win over her heart.

*For all my book girlies who dream
of being safely kidnapped—this one is for you.*

Author's Note

Dear, Reader!

Thank you for taking a chance on Tied Up for Love!

This book was written out of nothing but a dream, late nights, and a lot of caffeine. This book is a satirical, fun, and witty story about a dark romance reader and her unhinged inner thoughts, the kind that make her believe she can turn her captor into her book boyfriend. I hope you enjoy reading about the chaotic mess that is Charlie and Aiden as much as I loved writing it.

Tied Up for Love contains explicit language, kidnapping, grief of parental loss, parental loss (off screen). Please read with care.

With love,

Nora

Contents

1.	Charlie	1
2.	Aiden	7
3.	Charlie	11
4.	Aiden	15
5.	Charlie	19
6.	Aiden	25
7.	Charlie	31
8.	Aiden	35
9.	Charlie	39
10.	Aiden	43
11.	Charlie	47
12.	Aiden	53
13.	Charlie	59
14.	Aiden	63
15.	Charlie	69
16.	Aiden	73
17.	Charlie	79
18.	Aiden	83
19.	Charlie	89
20.	Charlie	95
	Epilogue	101
	Review	105
	Acknowledgments	107
	About the Author	109
	Also by Nora Lane	111

MAPLE DINER
Everly Falls, OK
POSTCARD
I THINK I'M FALLING FOR MY KIDNAPPER!
CHARLIE'S
BATTER CO.
LED UP FOR LOVE
17

Chapter 1

Charlie

The sack over my head smells like off-brand laundry detergent and questionable life choices, which is honestly very on theme for my life.

"Oh my god," I whisper into the darkness. "Is this...a kidnapping?"

Of course, on the one day I promise myself I'll relax and let my guard down, this happens.

Today is supposed to be easy. Low stress. Maybe even fun.

I've been running myself ragged the last few weeks with my microbakery, Charlie's Batter Co. From early mornings to late nights, flour in my hair, butter under my fingernails, and dishes covered in sourdough. They pile high in my sink, orders stacked up so high that my little kitchen looks like the set of *The Great British Bake Off: Panic Edition*. Between sourdough loaves, custom cookie boxes, and Mrs. Thomason's third "emergency" lemon cake of the month, I am barely keeping my head above buttercream.

Not that I mind, exactly. I love it. After the mountain of rejection emails I got from every Montessori school in the metro, moving back home to Everly Falls and starting my small microbakery felt like the breath of fresh air I desperately needed.

My small town is nestled between rolling hills and a canopy of old oak and maple trees, the kind that turn Main Street into a tunnel of gold and crimson every fall—the perfect backdrop for those Hallmark movies.

No matter where you've been, the community here will always be there for you. They have a way of folding you back and reminding you who you are when everything else feels like it's spinning off course. I thought a degree in early childhood development was my calling, but now I'm not so sure.

Baking has been my little haven, keeping me grounded from all the what-ifs. It started as a little experiment in my small kitchen, something to do to keep my mind and hands busy. I didn't expect the success I would have from it. It helps that my town was determined to see me succeed. What began with a few locals ordering sourdough loaves then blossomed into a full-blown online business when my best friend, Jade, used her marketing skills to grow my online presence. Now, I manage online orders, feature in a few online articles, and am the town's official baker. It is small, but it's turning into something that is actually growing. Something that I am proud of. Something I call *my own*.

I'm saving every spare dollar, tucking it away, because one day soon, I'm going to trade in the chaos of my cramped apartment kitchen for a storefront in the heart of Main Street—right next to The Lantern Nook, our local bookstore. This way, all the book lovers like myself can come and enjoy a sweet treat while diving into the worlds of brooding mafia men. *A girl can dream.*

But for now, I need a break. The stress of keeping up with the orders by myself and the knowledge of a vacancy available for my shop has been keeping me up at night. I'm on my second cup of coffee this morning and it's only eight am. A relaxing morning is long overdue, and nothing screams "relaxing morning" more than walking down Main Street.

I love this time of year in Everly Falls. The hustle and bustle of Main Street as the town prepares for our annual Christmas in the Falls. The sun is peaking through this morning, providing some warmth to a normally frosty morning. The cold front creates the perfect nip in the air. Storefront windows glow warmly against the cool breeze, and twinkling lights hang from every tree and awning, making it impossible not to enjoy the morning.

It's the perfect morning for my outing with Claire at the town's bookstore. Mrs. Whitaker has been running the place since I was a toddler, coming in for Saturday story time with my mom. She is like a second grandmother to me, and I still try to visit a few times a month, especially since her grandson and only living relative hasn't been back since he left for his town. Something tells me that when he finally does, things in Everly Falls won't be the same, but that's not my story to share.

Who's Claire, you might ask. Claire is my built-in forever ride or die. Being an identical twin does that to you. She was born only three minutes before me, but she acts like the "older" sister—always on me about making sure I eat, having clean clothes, and lately, carving out time for myself. She is a big believer in taking care of your mental health, and I am so thankful she's looking out for me. That's the beauty of having a twin; they have a sixth sense about what you need.

Now, if only other habits of hers rubbed off on me. Claire has always been the "put-together" one. She knew early on she wanted to be a sports photographer and worked tirelessly to get there. The girl even has her whole life mapped out on an Excel sheet. When she made me a budget tracker for my microbakery, I lasted two days before deleting it. The anxiety it gave me was not worth it. To this day, she still doesn't know

I'm basically flying blind with my business. Future Charlie can deal with tax season when it comes.

And yes, you heard that right. Claire and Charlie. Or Charlotte, if we're using my government name. Our parents thought matching names were adorable. As we got older, though, the Bennett twins were anything but identical. Sure, we both inherited our mom's chestnut hair, chocolate-brown eyes, high cheekbones, and were lucky to receive her olive-toned complexion as biracial children of a Vietnamese mother and African American father, but that's where the similarities end.

Claire is reserved and demure; she takes Pilates classes, goes on hot girl walks, and makes sure only the best goes into her body—minus the occasional sourdough chocolate chip cookies she'll eat when stressed. Me, on the other hand, well, I'm more of a do-what-makes-you-happy person. And cardio? Does not make me happy. Sourdough fudge brownies? Definitely makes me happy. I'm not as toned as Claire, but I do try to make the occasional trip to the gym when time allows. I have to at least offset the sugar intake from taste testing my own creations.

Ever since I moved back home, we've been seeing less and less of each other with her busier schedule. She had a huge piece take off when she captured the perfect angle of a player going down during an injury at the annual Eagleton University versus Brooksdale Medical Center charity flag football. Her boss, Mick, has been sending her to more in-person sporting events. I can't wait to catch her up on everything. She's doing amazing at work, and her love life is thriving with her new boyfriend, Eli.

Unlike me, I turned twenty-six in August this year, and honestly? My life looks nothing like the Pinterest board I once made for myself.

No job. No husband. No family of my own. Not a single prospect insight.

By now, I thought I'd at least have one of those boxes checked. The only man in my life is Doughbi-Wan, my little sourdough starter, the heart of my microbakery. Without him, I wouldn't be here. He is the one constant in my life. Real men let you down—ask my previous boyfriends.

Wait, what is happening again? Oh, right, being kidnapped.

Chapter 2

Aiden

Bringing my hand over my face, I try to shield the sun from my eyes on this crisp morning as I exhale and contemplate my life decision. The sun is just peeking through the gray clouds and wrapping me in a fleeting warmth. I'm sitting outside The Crimson Cup, a small coffee shop on the corner of Main Street, taking a sip of my white chocolate peppermint mocha. I know, it sounds like a total girlie drink, but when the barista said it was like a warm Christmas hug, I couldn't resist. I get enough black coffee at the hospital to last a lifetime, so when I finally escape for a cup, I let myself indulge in whatever the season's hyped-up treat happens to be.

This part of town is nice, now that it's morning and I can see Main Street better. I walked Main Street last night to do some reconnaissance of the area, trying to figure out the best place to snatch her. Storefronts are decorated with wreaths and garlands, and the soft hum of holiday music floats through the air. It has a sort of Hallmark charm, making it calm, cozy, and inviting. The scent of fresh palms lingers in the air, a breath of calm I needed from the busy, bustling city life. Between long hours at the hospital, weekends volunteering, residency applications, and taking care of my new puppy, Jake, I am exhausted. All I want is a nice, relaxing weekend, which begs the question of why I agreed to this kidnapping ploy.

Outside the coffee shop, a couple walks hand in hand into the boutique, and children giggle as they dodge around people hustling down the sidewalk. This is the perfect day to execute this kidnapping; the town's annual *Christmas in the Falls* prep is in full swing, and with the crowd, I can easily get to her without anyone noticing.

Sipping my coffee, I savor the sweetness of white chocolate pairing perfectly with the peppermint note—the barista was right, this is like Christmas in a cup. I scan up and down the streets out of habit, my eyes darting between the shops and crowd when I spot her prancing toward the bookstore.

She looks exactly the way Eli described, dressed in the stereotypical book girl clothing. She has on dark green tights, aka God's gift to men, an oversized tee that boldly declares "I'm Booked (By the Mafia Don)" and hangs off one shoulder, and a cream tote with a knife logo and the slogan "Ride It" that bounces against her hip.

The second my gaze lands on her, something in me goes still. Like the air between us thickens. My pulse stutters, then hammers hard enough to feel it in my throat. She radiates warmth and sunshine; I can almost feel it reaching me across the street. An air of carefree surrounds her, instantly drawing me into her orbit.

She's chatting away on her phone, looking effortlessly beautiful, like she rolled out of bed without a care in the world. A messy bun is perched on her head, with strands of chestnut hair slipping free and catching the breeze. I imagine what they'd feel like between my fingers, probably soft and silky. Even from here, her big brown eyes draw me in. Her light olive skin looks impossibly soft—touchable. I can't take my eyes off her. She's *captivating*. Then she laughs, the sound bright, unguarded, and burrowing under my skin. I drag in a slow, cool breath, the scent of roasted coffee and autumn leaves doing nothing to settle the tight pull in my chest. I have no business looking at her like this, because she's *not mine*.

Glancing around, I take in the flow of people walking by. My time in the service taught me to always be aware of my surroundings. On the other hand, this girl has zero self-awareness, so lost in her phone call that she nearly walks straight into a lamppost. A kind older woman reaches out, tapping her arm just in time to save her from the collision.

For a ridiculous second, a surge of protectiveness washes over me. It makes no sense, but the thought of anyone hurting her makes my jaw ache with anger. Which is insane, considering I'm about to be the creep who's about to snatch her in broad daylight.

I watch as she ends her call and walks closer to the bookstore entrance. I know my window to get her without anyone noticing is closing. It's now or never. I tug the neck gaiter up my face, just high enough to cover my nose. People have seen weirder things lately, but I'm still banking on no one questioning a six-four, built-like-an-ox guy in a skeleton neck gaiter walking down Main Street. I know, the skeleton isn't very conspicuous, but it was what I found in the back of my closet.

With precision and purpose, I cross the street and make my way to the alley nestled between the bookstore and a vacant store. I make my movement quick, smooth, and decisive, like executing a flawless covert operation with my men. One arm around her waist, the other hand covering her mouth, just in case she screams. Her body stiffens beneath me, but there's no fight. I drag her back into the shadows of the alley, my heart pounding so hard I swear the people sitting outside the coffee shop can hear.

I wrap my legs around her, pinning her to my chest. With my free hand, I yank the potato sack from my back pocket and slip it over her head just as I hear her whisper breathlessly, "Oh my god. Is this...a kidnapping?"

Chapter 3

Charlie

My adrenaline is pumping. I can feel the blood rush to my ears. *Calm down, Charlie, freaking out is not going to help.* I take a deep breath, counting to four before I exhale. How could I have been so careless? I blame Lila and Jade; I was on the phone with them, caught up in our usual shenanigans. I must not have been as aware of my surroundings.

Lila and Jade are my oldest and dearest friends. They're practically honorary sisters to Claire and me; we went through our awkward teenage years together and stayed close even after heading off to different colleges. When Lila moved in with her grandma after her parents passed away, Claire and I took it upon ourselves to look after her. She was a year younger than us but folded perfectly into our existing trio with Jade. Jade was born a month after Claire and me in the same hospital, even delivered by the same nurse. Growing up, we were the three musketeers until Lila joined, making us the Fantastic Four.

As we got older, catching up has been so hard, especially with Lila being a flight attendant and always on the go. We rarely got to catch up with all of us. Prime example, Claire couldn't join the call this morning. My head was in the clouds thinking about Lila living out a real-life, love-at-first-sight trope while on a work trip.

And now, I'm in my own real-life trope. Captor and captive. If this was a dark romance book, instant swoon. However, it's likely not, and I probably should figure out how to get free before I end up in a Netflix documentary. Focusing all the brain cells I have left on the situation, I try to regain some sense of awareness. My brain struggles to compute that I am being kidnapped in Everly Falls. Not *our* little town.

Then I remember, this is our busiest time of the year and the town is swarming with out-of-towners. Today is the first day of our annual *Christmas in the Falls*, a week-long tradition where the entire town transforms into something out of a snow globe. Main Street drips with twinkle lights, every store-front competes in the annual window-decorating contest, and the scent of pecan-covered cinnamon sugar and hot cocoa lingers in the air twenty-four seven. Tourists come from all over the state just to experience it, and tonight is the inaugural lighting of the Christmas tree. The tree is the largest fresh-cut Christmas tree in the world at 140 feet tall. It's like someone stole the tree out of Whoville from The Grinch.

The strong arms holding me against a broad chest squeeze, reminding me I am about to be taken—and not in a good way. I inhale. I don't know why, but obviously, what else should you do in these moments? It smells like smoke and cedar. How cliché. It's like he walked into Dillard's and said, "I would like a bottle of your oversold, overpriced cologne. One that screams, *I'm your next book boyfriend.*" He does have a hint of another smell—aftershave? Oooh, maybe he has a beard. I'm a sucker for a man with a beard. There's just something about the scruff grazing over different parts of my body that heightens my arousal. That's an untimely thought; maybe now's not the time to think about your arousal.

Okay, think, Charlie. How would the badass FMC from every dark romance novel we devour get out of this? She'd outsmart her captor with her wit and banter her way into his heart. Now, if I'm lucky, I'll have the same faith, and he won't just be my captor but my next boyfriend. I'm internally laughing at myself for that unhinged thought, but when he shoves me into the backseat of the car, I can't help but shout, "Enemies to lovers, baby!" as I throw my hands up like I'm on a rollercoaster at Disneyland.

He immediately yanks them down, pulling them behind me, and I feel a rope biting into my skin. Oh, *kinky.* Maybe he's into bondage play. The door slams shut, and I hear his footsteps receding. Taking a calming deep breath, I fumble around my surroundings. Soft leather seats. Crisp, clean car smell. Not exactly what I imagined for a kidnapping. Wouldn't kidnappers drive something gross? You know, stale fast-food wrappers, smoke-stained upholstery, and maybe a faint whiff of despair? This car is nice. Expensive, even. Which can only mean one thing: the mafia is involved.

I wonder if he is Russian? Better yet, I wonder why me? My brain flips through every romance trope I've ever read. Maybe he spotted me across the street, instantly captivated. Or maybe I bumped into him at the market, he became obsessed, stalked me for weeks, and now he is finally ready to claim what is his. Ooooh. I like that one the best. Fingers crossed, that is my arc. At least, that is the best-case scenario, because if he were obsessed with me, I could use that to turn him into my dream guy. Classic case of "I can fix him." I could totally change him. He just needs a little guidance, a spark of inspiration from his muse—me—to turn his life around. We'll live happily ever after, and this will be the meet-cute we'll tell our children. Our "How I Met Your Mother" story. *This isn't like the books, though*, I scold myself. I may not have dated anyone in months, but I'm not that desperate. I need to focus. Figure out how to get out of this situation.

The driver's car door slams, and the engine rumbles to life. I shift in the seat, straightening my spine like a pro. I've prepared for this moment. Not literally—I don't exactly tie myself up often—but mentally, emotionally, spiritually? Oh, I'm ready.

I've read enough dark romance novels to recognize every red flag in the book, and I'm confident I can spin them to my advantage. If this guy is going to ruin my Saturday morning, he is going to earn it. Time to weaponize tropes.

If I know anything about the Captor Arc, their heroes are usually grumpy and hate life. And if they are grumpy, the best way to pry them open is relentless, insistent conversation. It's like I've been training my whole life for this. My mom used to say I overshared when I was nervous. It was a terrible habit, especially when you are already awkward and decide to reminisce about getting your period at a seventh-grade pool party and how a friend had to coach you through shoving a tampon up your hoo-haa from outside the bathroom door.

I probably won't share that story with him. But there are plenty of others to share.

Okay, tall, dark, and handsome kidnapper. Let's see where our story takes us

Chapter 4

Aiden

I slide into the driver's seat like this is any other car ride. I've been working hard to keep my head level during all the stressful calls at the hospital, an important characteristic a physician must have under pressure. Add that to my years in the service, and I am the picture of calm, cool, collected. I've captured way harder targets in my career, this five-four brunette is a piece of cake. Still, I can't help thinking back to the night my best friend, Eli, cooked up this half-assed idea, because if this goes south, it won't be my first time cleaning up someone else's bad decision.

* * *

"Come on, man," Eli says, handing me another cold beer.

Eli has been my best friend since high school. I wasn't the most open guy, I know, shocker, but when this scrawny, nerdy kid showed up in my homeroom, I didn't expect him to be exactly what I needed. He had this easy smile and way of laughing at himself that chipped away at my walls before I realized it. We bonded over late-night gaming sessions, somewhere between trash-talking while playing Mario Kart, running laps around the school track, and wiping out all the cones during driving school. He went from being "the new kid" to my best friend.

His dad was in the military, like mine, which meant Eli was used to bouncing around, never really planting roots. Similar to me. I think that's why he held on to me so tightly, and in turn, I held on to him. He was the first person I ever trusted and confided in about my mom. We lost her when I was five, while my dad was on deployment. She was delivering Ava, my baby sister, and there were...complications.

Which was the reason why it was hard on my dad when I first told him about Eli and me enlisting. Eli talked about enlisting after high school graduation, following in his dad's footsteps, for as long as I could remember. Eli was first in line to sign up when the recruiter came, and I was second. My dad wasn't happy, seeing his only son leave and remembering the loss of his wife. It was a lot we both had to work through. In the end, he understood the bond Eli and I had, and he knew I needed to do it. It was something he and I both needed to work through our loss by facing our fears. I appreciated him and his support because it was the best decision I could've made. The Marines broke me down, built me back up, and showed me what kind of man I wanted to be. I came out stronger, sharper, and more focused.

Eli's blue eyes meet mine through the rim of his black glasses while running a hand through his dirty blonde hair. He's giving me that puppy dog eye like Jake does when he wants more peanut butter. The guy is built like an offensive lineman, with a wide chest, broad shoulders, and muscular arms. I've seen him take down five guys without batting an eye, but he's a big teddy bear, and when he wants something, he will turn on the charm.

Shit, I can feel myself caving.

Staring out into the backyard, I try to think up a polite excuse to get out of this weird request. I had been thinking about *tonight all day. I just wanted to relax and decompress on one of the rare, quiet evenings I'd had in a long time—no exams looming, no shifts at the hospital, no obligations. Yet, here I am discussing a potential kidnapping ruse with my best friend.*

"It's going to be hilarious," Eli says. "She's obsessed with those dark romance books—kidnapping tropes, mafia boyfriends, all that. She'll love it."

"You want me to commit a felony for laughs?" I ask, staring at him like he's lost his damn mind.

"It's not a felony if it's consensual," Eli shoots back, all smug confidence and zero sense. "Besides, she's expecting it. Think of it like immersive role play."

I blink at him. "Immersive—? You've officially lost it."

He just grins, like this is the most normal conversation in the world.

"Why can't you do it then?" My tone comes out equal parts confused and weary.

"Because she'll spot me coming a mile away," he says, like that's obvious. "She won't recognize you. You guys haven't actually met." He pauses, then smirks. "Which, by the way, is blasphemous considering you're my best friend. But I'll give you a pass, 'cause I know your rotation with Dr. Owens is brutal right now."

I pinch the bridge of my nose, already regretting letting him get this far into the pitch.

"And," he adds, leaning back like he's about to drop the final piece of his master plan, "I don't really know the layout of her hometown yet, so I need time to prepare."

I don't respond because, well, I don't know how to.

"Think of it as a vacation."

"A vacation?"

"Yeah, I'll get you a little Airbnb near Main Street. It's the Christmas in the Falls kick off this weekend, it'll be a good getaway from the hospital and residency applications."

"Right," I deadpan. *"Because nothing says a nice, relaxing vacation like accidental kidnapping charges."*

* * *

Everything made sense that night. Eli gave an enticing offer. Though maybe it was the two IPAs buzzing through my system—because right now, I'm questioning why in the hell I agreed to this ridiculous plan.

Chapter 5

Charlie

My head hit the side of the window as the car turned, hitting a pothole. "Ouch," I mumble beneath my breath. We must be leaving the parking lot. My mind replays the event, trying to remember any clue that could help me put together an escape plan.

I had finished my call with the girls and was putting away my phone before continuing my walk to The Lantern Nook. I looked down for a second when his arms came around my chest and a hand covered my mouth. Strong arms, great forearms—okay, so I felt him up a bit when he was hauling me toward the alleyway nestled between an empty storefront and commercial real estate office. It was the storefront I was going to check out for my bakery, which made sense why he dragged me behind the building toward the empty lot.

I remember a car, a blue electric sedan that I didn't recognize. I know everyone in town, and *no one* drives an electric car in this town. It only means one thing—this guy is definitely an out-of-towner.

I need to figure out how to get free. I have never been good with keeping calm under pressure. I usually overreact and this might be one of those situations that I should overreact. Maybe if I'm unhinged enough, he won't want to keep me. If I am going to pull off this plan, I have to act like I want to be here. Trick him into believing this is the best thing to ever happen to me. Reverse psychology, baby. Classic.

Crossing my legs, I prepare my arsenal with all the unrealistic dark romance stories I have read while praying my sister notices I am gone and doesn't chalk up my being late as a normal "Charlie event." I start with step one of my plan. Distraction via conversation.

"Okay, so let's just address the elephant in the room," I say, putting more chipper in my tone than I had. "You, mysterious masked man, have literally every red flag I could possibly want in a book boyfriend. Kidnapping, check. Silent and broody, check."

I wiggle to adjust the sack over my head from tickling my nose, waiting for any signs of life from him. Nothing. Not even a grunt.

"Okay, strong silent type, I see you," I say brightly.

"So," I say, trying to act nonchalant, "what's your tragic backstory? Mafia? Childhood trauma? Did your ex betray you with your sworn enemy? Please tell me you're not just, like, a random guy who got lost on his way to a gas station robbery, because that would ruin the vibe."

The man lets out the longest sigh I've ever heard in my life. Like he regrets not just kidnapping me but also being born. Good, it is working. Time to dial up the unhinged meter.

"Honestly," I press on, teeth chattering from the cold, "if I d-don't develop Stockholm Syndrome by chapter f-five, I'll be disappointe-d-d. Don't let me d-down." The chill of the first cold front seeping through the car makes me regret not putting on a jacket before I left my apartment.

You could hear a pin drop in this car, but then the sound of the vent blasts through the silence. I can feel the heat enveloping me in a warm hug. My lip curves up in a small smile—aw, he notices. That's kind of sweet. Maybe he isn't so bad after all. *Said every true crime victim before they got murdered.* Right. I can't let my guard down.

What else could I throw at him? Something that would make any man's eye twitch, but women would eat up with a spoon. Oh. Gossip!

"Speaking of disappointments," I chirp, feeling much warmer than before, "do you have a radio in this thing? Like, if you're going to abduct me, the least you can do is give me some tunes. Preferably Taylor Swift. Actually—did you hear she got engaged?!"

Still nothing. I'm starting to worry this plan might not work. What if he's immovable? Stubborn. Unflinching. Oh god, is this how I die? My body, found in an alley, next to my Kindle. OH MY GOD, my Kindle! The book content there, the cops would see it, they would go through my library and see all my books. No, absolutely not. I have to trust that Claire would know better and delete all my history before they got to it.

"Oh my god, you haven't, have you?" I gasp. "This is huge news! Taylor Swift is engaged! Can you imagine the wedding? The dress? The guest list? I'm telling you, if she doesn't release a secret double album as wedding favors, I'm writing her a strongly worded DM."

The man exhales so hard I think the windshield might fog up. I'm getting to him. This is perfect. I continue rambling, all while using my foot to feel around for my bag. I could have sworn I heard him drop it on the floor of the car. I remember because I heard my Kindle thunk and a little part of myself died. I can get hurt, my bruises will heal, but not my Kindle. Not my baby.

I spent months scraping away, saving for the newest edition, the color soft. I wanted to see those pretty covers in bright, vibrant colors. I told myself if I could see the pretty cover on my Kindle, I wouldn't buy the physical books. *The lies I tell myself.* In my defense, I have bought fewer physical copies. I've moved on to the special editions! The ones that are coveted by the bookish community. The ones that if I got robbed by a book lover, that would be what they steal. What can I say? We're special ones.

"You're quiet," I say. "Which is fine, broody is hot, don't get me wrong. But this is a long drive, and I don't want us to miss a bonding opportunity. Think about it—we could be besties by the time we get to your creepy abandoned warehouse and/or mansion. If you're planning to chain me up in a basement, you should know I am very particular about basement decor."

I step on something hard and internally wince—my poor Kindle. I wiggle left and right, trying to slyly reach my tote bag. With my hands bound behind my back, this simple task is nearly impossible. I'm holding my breath at every shift. I can't get caught before my plan even takes off. Feeling for the bag with my shoes, I angle my body sideways to lean toward the strap of my tote. I bite the inside of my cheek, fully concentrating on hooking the strap with my fingers.

Finally, after what feels like an eternity, I manage to hook a corner of the strap under my bound hands. It's awkward, uncomfortable, and I nearly drop it twice, but inch by excruciating inch, I pull it up behind me. My heart hammers in my chest, and I swear I'm going to pass out from holding my breath for so long.

Keeping the chatter up so he doesn't get suspicious, I start to think about all the mafia hero starter packs. "By the way, how's your knife collection? You have one, right? Dark romance guys always have one. Or guns."

The car hits a bump. I bounce in my seat, grinning like a kid on a carnival ride. Oh, he's flustered, this is good!

"Wait—are you allergic to cats? Because that would be a dealbreaker for me, personally."

Nothing. Man, is this guy alive or did a robot kidnap me?

"You know," I continue, "this is kind of romantic. Just you, me, and the open road. Classic captor-captive setup. Ten out of ten. No notes."

I wiggle both hands in my tote bag, feeling around for my phone. The rope around my wrists makes every movement awkward—like I am trying to pinch things with crab claws. As I rummage through what feels like an endless pit of junk, I can't help thinking maybe my mom is right for nicknaming my bag Narnia.

Chapter 6

Aiden

Does this girl ever stop talking?

The answer is no.

She's been babbling nonstop since I put her in the car, words tumbling out like she's auditioning for an audiobook deal about her own kidnapping. Her voice echoes through the car cabin, and it's obnoxiously delightful.

I have not met Claire before, and from what Eli has told me about her, his description seems a bit different. That's a mild way to put it. This girl is made up of rainbows and sunshine. You can tell in her voice that she could find a silver lining in any situation. Case in point, she seems to actually be enjoying this kidnapping.

Maybe because she's on to me. Like she knows this is the "immersive role playing" they've planned before. I decide silence is my best bet. Ignoring her is easier than engaging. If I don't engage, I won't give anything away and may make it out of this kidnapping unscathed.

She has been talking a mile a minute, never pausing long enough for my brain to catch up. I swear I haven't heard her take a breath. It's actually impressive. I wonder if there's a case study on how long females can talk without breaking to breathe. Like what would her lung capacity be.

Wow. Maybe Eli is right, I do need this vacation.

I grip the wheel tighter, focusing on the traffic that has built up in the last ten minutes. I can smell the faint burn of brakes from the traffic behind us, hear the muffled honks and murmurs of people walking Main Street.

Well, this isn't the quick getaway I had hoped for. Literally anyone can look in at the liability I have sitting in the back seat with a sack over her head. My mind is busy trying to figure out how to be incognito when her next question jolts me from my thoughts.

"By the way, how's your knife collection? You have one, right? Dark romance guys always have one. Or guns."

My knife collection? This girl is certified insane. Is this what drew Eli to her? He needed a little insanity in his life? I chuckle to myself. I can imagine all kinds of misfits this girl can get into. A wave of unexpected jealousy washes over me. I can't pinpoint if I'm jealous of the relationship or that he has *her.* I don't know what it is about her but there's just something I can't seem to put my finger on.

I can't even remember the last time I've been on a real date and connected with someone. Medical school doesn't leave much room for that kind of thing. And no one has ever caught my attention enough to make me want to put in the extra effort. Most nights, I'm too tired to care. My brain is always half calculating, half worrying—exams, rotations, volunteering. The late nights of studying and the early morning rotations all blur together into one long, exhausting string that has become my new normal.

I wish I had a special someone constant in my life. Someone I can come home to and let all the bad from the day melt away with. I want someone who's there when I walk through the door—ready to listen to the gory details after a long shift in the ER, excited about the newborn I helped deliver, and willing to lend a quiet ear when I lose a patient to lung cancer.

Her over-the-top sigh pulls me back to our conversation. She's leaning back on the headrest, the picture of relaxation. "This is kind of romantic. Just you, me, and the open road. Classic captor-captive setup. Ten out of ten. No notes." The way she giggles at her own commentary has me shaking my head at how ridiculous this whole situation is.

I come to a stop at the intersection as a young family is making their way through the crosswalk. A tall, skinny guy, likely my age, is trying to keep his toddler from touching the hood of my car as they pass by. I hold my breath, hoping they don't glance in too deep and notice the girl with the sack over her head. Luckily for me, the dad is too distracted trying to keep his toddler in check to even look my way.

Desperate to appear nonchalant, I turn my body to the back seat, avoiding eye contact with any more pedestrians. If I don't see them, they don't see me. It worked with playground hide-and-seek, so it should work now.

There's one flaw in my decision to avert gazes from passersby; I'm now looking directly at my captive. I was too focused on executing the mission earlier that I didn't really have time to see her—and now I can. Her face is breathtaking, there's no denying it. But her body is just as alluring. I can't help but notice every curve of her body. Her oversized sweater slips off one shoulder, revealing the delicate line of her collarbone, and all I can think about is pressing soft kisses there. The thought hits me hard and unwelcome. What the hell? This is *Eli's girlfriend.*

I turn back around, avoiding dissecting into why I was checking out Eli's girlfriend when I notice her fidgeting out of the corner of my eye, her body angling toward the window, like she's trying to make a break for it. I click the lock button to confirm she's secured in the car. I try to think of anything but the girl tied up in my back seat but like a moth to a flame, I can't help but steal glances at her from my rearview mirror. Even under that oversized sweater, I can tell she isn't stick-thin like the fitness-obsessed girls at the gym, but soft in all the right ways—curves that hint she doesn't shy away from dessert, and small, perky breasts that would fit perfectly in my hands. *What has gotten into me? Who has thoughts like that about their best friend's girlfriend?*

The cars are inching forward at snail's pace. At this rate, I'll be late meeting Eli at the drop-off. This girl continues to chatter about mafia boyfriends and Taylor Swift, oblivious to my internal turmoil. The more she talks, the more I can't seem to shake this uncontrollable feeling that draws me to her, like the irresistible pull of the tides. As if she can feel me staring, she shifts her posture to angle toward the front. "Are you glaring at me right now? I bet you are. You've got that whole silent, brooding aura. I can feel it. Ooooh, are we doing the enemies-to-lovers thing? That's the ultimate trope."

I bite back a laugh at this girl's bravado. Here she is getting kidnapped, and yet she's acting like it's a normal Saturday morning to be tied up in the back of someone's car.

"I just want you to know, I've always been ready for this moment. Like, spiritually prepared. Some girls dream about prom or their wedding day. Me? I've fantasized about this exact scenario. Tied up by a mystery man in the back of his car on the way to what I hope is a remote cabin—preferably one with Wi-Fi, so I can still download my Kindle Unlimited books. Honestly, it's a dream come true. Who doesn't want to be locked up in a remote cabin with no one to bother them and unlimited amounts of reading time? I mean, the sack could've been silk instead of burlap, but I'll let that slide."

Hearing her say she prepared for this causes a wave of protectiveness to roll through me. The thought of her being tied up in the back of another guy's car has my grip on the wheel tightening, my knuckles turning bone white, and I exhale through my nose, sharp and uneven. My heart is sprinting like I'm back in basic training.

She sighs happily, settling back against the seat.

"Don't worry, I've read so many mafia romances. I know exactly how this works. You threaten me, I sass you, you brood, we kiss—boom. Instant bestsellers!"

Chapter 7

Charlie

As discreetly as I can, I fumble for my phone, my fingers brushing over the smooth screen before I awkwardly pull it from the tote. Dropping it on the outside of my thigh near the door, I hope he can't see it from his angle.

Okay. Step one, secure lifeline—done.

Now what? I didn't think this through; I still have this sack over my head. How am I supposed to use facial recognition? I hate that the new upgrade to this phone took away the Touch ID recognition feature. I should definitely write a strongly worded letter about how that feature could save my life—better yet, if I get out of here alive, I will sue.

My nose itches under this sack. He couldn't get a better material? I mean, you would think the Russian mafia could afford a silk sack. Wait, is he Russian? I guess since he's not talking to me, I can't tell what ethnicity he is. If only he would take this off so I could hover my face over my phone. By now, I'm sure I've sweated through it, and my mascara is smearing. No way would facial recognition pick up a trash panda—aka raccoon—as the owner of this phone.

Okay, time for plan B. Or as my favorite *Friends* character would say, *"PIVOT!"*

Our car lurches forward, then abruptly stops. We've been in this pattern for a good five minutes. I bet traffic is already a nightmare this morning with all the preparation for the festival. With out-of-towners coming in and the locals getting their storefront ready, I'm guesstimating we're still crawling down Main Street. I'm internally praying someone sees me, jumps out in front of this car, and stops my captor. Keeping my voice casual, trying to hide any panic, I start my next mission to remove this scratchy sack.

"Alright, let's get into something important—murder. Be honest. Have you, or have you not, killed a man with your bare hands?" I say, knowing this question would rattle anyone, even a seasoned mafia enforcer. The car jerks just slightly. Bingo. I grin underneath my sack.

"Don't worry, I'm not judging," I say sweetly. "In fact, I'm hoping for a yes. Because, babe, if you haven't at least snapped a neck or two in a dimly lit alleyway, you're not really commitment material." I sound ridiculous even to my own ears, but I'm committed now; I have to figure out how to get out of this situation.

I can feel the irritation thrumming from the driver's seat. We're at peak annoyance.

"Ugh, traffic," I groan, letting the complaint roll out like I don't care. "This totally ruins the vibe. Can't you just swerve onto the shoulder and do something illegal? You're supposed to be a dangerous man, right? Break some laws for me."

I can hear the faint melody of Christmas music—probably coming from one of those pop-up speakers the town installs every holiday season. Confirmation of my theory that we haven't gotten far.

The scent of roasted pecan and cinnamon sugar sneaks in through the vents. The situation is almost absurd. Outside, people are probably sipping cocoa and taking selfies under twinkling lights, while I'm tied up, covered in a sack, and sitting behind a man who could either be my captor or a plot twist waiting to happen.

I refuse to be the damsel in distress.

"HELP! I'M BEING KIDNAPPED!" I scream.

My body jerks forward as he suddenly slams on the brake. I smirk under the sack. He is definitely flustered now.

"Okay, that was uncalled for. You could give a girl a little warning before you stop so abruptly." I just have to play it cool—nonchalant, like this isn't affecting me and I'm not over here overanalyzing that I'm in a non-matching bra and panties for when the coroner does my autopsy.

"I'm kidding! But seriously, I think we both know it looks shady as fuck for me to be sitting in the back of your car with a sack over my head. Just take the sack off. I'm tied up, what will I do?"

I wait with bated breath, wondering if I said and asked too much. I don't know how much longer we have in this car. I don't even know anything about him. Provoking him might not be the way to go. I sigh to myself; this is just like me, diving headfirst into a crazy plan before fully thinking about the consequences.

Like when I thought I could open a romance mobile bookstore and travel around the city doing pop-ups. I was knee-deep in Pinterest boards and business plans, already picturing myself as the quirky romance-only mobile bookstore of everyone's dreams—until I realized those retro vans cost more than my student loans. Add on the renovation costs to make sure books didn't go flying every time I hit a pothole, and that dream flatlined one night over a pint of Blue Bell.

Pushing that negativity from my mind. I will not die; not today, Satan!

I lean forward. "Do you have mommy issues? You can tell me. It's practically a requirement."

He groans. A real, audible groan. I squeal in triumph. "There it is! A vocal response! This is progress. We're bonding."

Silence.

"You know, this car ride is basically our slow-burn enemies-to-lovers arc." I tilt my head.

"Unless, of course, you're more of a hate-fuck first, love later kind of guy. Which, to be clear, I would also accept. In fact, it's highly encouraged."

Chapter 8

Aiden

I rub my hand down my face, letting out a frustrated groan. This girl is impossible. Between the traffic, her incessant talking, and the fear of getting caught, my blood pressure is probably through the roof.

If I don't keep my head straight, I'm definitely going to jail.

As if she can hear my inner monologue, the girl chooses that exact moment to belt out: "HELP! I'M BEING KIDNAPPED!"

I nearly swerve onto the sidewalk.

She giggles, the sound warm and inviting. Slightly unhinged, like she knows exactly what she's doing to me.

"I'm kidding! But seriously, I think we both know it looks shady as fuck for me to be sitting in the back of your car with a sack over my head. Just take the sack off. I'm tied up, what will I do?"

I contemplate the idea. A nagging voice in the back of my head reminds me she's right, and I have no idea how long this traffic will last.

An old couple walking their little Yorkie reminds me of

Jake. I hope Eli remembers to put him back in his crate before he leaves. I can't afford to keep replacing my socks. I groan just thinking of the mountains of socks I had to replace.

"There it is! A vocal response! This is progress. We're bonding."

Wait, what did she say? What are we bonding over?

"You know, this car ride is basically our slow-burn enemies-to-lovers arc." The muffle of her voice makes me wonder if she realizes her talking is decreasing the amount of air she has in there. Instinctively, I start to think about all the biological factors she's under. The stress hormones from being kidnapped, the low oxygen exchange from the thick mask, the—

"Unless, of course, you're more of a hate-fuck first, love later kind of guy. Which, to be clear, I would also accept. In fact, it's highly encouraged."

My eyes widen, like one of those cartoon characters, at her last comment. Did she just say *hate-fuck?*

The image of her on her back in the back seat, underneath me, moaning my name, has heat building low. I pinch the bridge of my nose, questioning my sanity. Has this girl put a hex on me? Because everything that comes out of her mouth is making me question my friendship with Eli. I wonder how mad he would be if I *kept* his girlfriend? I'm going with, super mad.

Traffic is slowly clearing and I thank every deity out there for speeding this kidnapping ruse along. Eli wasn't joking when he said the locals really did take their *Christmas in the Falls* event seriously. This traffic is no joke. Eli had warned me about the town's obsession with putting together a Hallmark-esque event, but I hadn't truly expected this. The streets are lined with twinkling lights wrapped around every lamppost, storefronts draped in garlands and oversized red bows. The aroma of roasted chestnuts, hot cocoa, and cinnamon wafts from the storefronts.

Cars inch past us, moving faster than before, but I can still sense eyes lingering on my car, scanning, judging, probably wondering why some guy is wearing a mask while driving. One minivan full of kids straight-up points at me, their wide eyes glued to the back seat. I adjust my posture, trying to look casual. Just a normal guy. Definitely not transporting a human being with a sack over her head. Nope. Just out for a drive. Maybe running errands. A very slow, very public, completely suspicious errand. My car's tinted windows help, but they're not magical. Even behind the darkness, anyone leaning close enough or with a curious mind could peek inside and spot her.

Once again, my mind wanders back to the girl. I can't help but picture her underneath the sack, probably grinning like the Cheshire cat at the possibility of her captor taking her to a remote location for some rest and relaxation. From the way she's leaning forward, her eyes are probably sparkling with absolute chaos. I clamp down on the urge to smile, forcing myself to focus on the road ahead.

She continues to chatter on, something about an enemies-to-lovers arc. I hate that her absurdly perfect, irritatingly fangirl voice makes me want to respond to her. She's so animated and excited, even in this ridiculous situation. The more she talks, the more I realize how dull and lonely my life has been. I don't think I've had a solid conversation with anyone that was not part of my job in months.

I'm thirty-four years old, about to head into my residency year where any social life is non-existent, and I have no other person to rely on outside of Eli. Medical school has taken all my free time. Yet, it's not a decision I'd ever change. Just like I knew in my gut that enlisting was the right thing to do, I knew going into medicine was my calling. The eight years I spent in the Marines, watching my guys get patched up by the Navy corpsmen both on and off the field, made me realize there was more I could do. Eli felt the same way, so once we had finished our last tour, we dove right into getting our licenses. It was tough; late nights, early mornings. We weren't in our primes like the other students but we had the drive. It was great having my brother with me, going through all the same struggles and relying on each other.

But recently, there's been a shift. Eli's spending more time with his girlfriend, confiding in and relying on her. It's not that I'm jealous. Well, maybe just a little jealous. I want that special someone to share life's highs and lows with. I want to curl up on the couch and watch trashy TV while eating our weight in ice cream. As I imagine the scenario in my head, I realize the person I picture on the couch with me is the girl in the back seat.

The thought hits me like a ton of bricks.

I am so in over my head.

Shaking my head from the unwelcome vision, I imagine the consequences of this kidnapping prank gone wrong. Getting caught by a cop. Arrested. The headlines. "Local man kidnapped girlfriend of best friend; claims he was coerced into an immersive role-playing ruse." Failing medical school because of a criminal record. My entire future flushed down a toilet over a "harmless prank."

Chapter 9

Charlie

My captor has gone completely radio silent.

Maybe it wasn't a good idea to suggest "hate-fuck," but I got nervous so I started rambling. I can tell traffic is starting to open up, and I need him to take this sack off so I can use my phone.

Lost in my pity party and self-doubt, I'm taken aback when a rush of fresh air hits my face. My eyes blink rapidly as the sudden rush of light assaults my vision. I'm temporarily blinded before my eyes adjust, and that's when I see him. Or, well, his side profile.

I wonder what made him change his mind to remove my sack. Must be my charming personality. I stare at my captor, who's in a simple black hoodie and a skeleton neck gaiter, hiding most of his face. His eyes are focused on the road ahead, and I can't get a good read on him.

I take inventory of my surroundings. The car interior is shockingly pristine. Black leather seats, spotless, the surfaces immaculate, not a speck of dust in sight. This guy would hate my little Civic. I mean, it's my version of clean; an empty cardboard box sitting in my passenger seat serves as my trash can for everything I drag in.

My eyes slowly drift to the rearview mirror where a hospital badge swings gently, catching the light. I lean forward, hoping to catch a glimpse of his name. The movement makes him glance back, and I freeze. His sharp gaze follows mine, and before I can think, his hand is on the badge. In one swift motion, he snatches it from the mirror and tosses it into the side compartment of his driver-side door. Well, there goes getting his name for the police report.

Remembering my escape plan, I fumble for my phone now that the sack is off. Awkwardly tapping at the black screen, waiting for it to turn on. Nothing happens. Did it die? No, no, no. I swear I left it on the charger last night. My pulse picks up. I can feel it against my ribs as my panic level rises. I take a shaky breath, willing my nerves to take a back seat so my brain can think. Freaking out won't help my phone turn on.

With my hands bound behind my back, it feels like I'm lifting imaginary weights as I try to get my phone into position. Oddly, the rope isn't tight. It's like he put it on more for show than to restrain me. I can move my wrists back and forth, so maybe I can actually get it off. Squeezing my hands into tight fists, I start to wiggle them back and forth. The rope gives just a little.

I unclench my hand and keep wiggling, remembering that one drunken night I got my hand stuck in a mason jar at Cadillac Ranch, the local bar in town. To be fair, some guy had called me chubby, and in my very tipsy state, I spotted the empty maraschino cherry jar behind the bar and proudly declared, "Oh yeah? Could a chubby girl fit her hand in this tiny jar?" Then I shoved my hand in and held it up in triumph. The guy walked away without another word, probably because he didn't know what to say. As soon as he was gone, though, I realized my mistake. I was completely stuck. Claire and I spent the next ten minutes wiggling and pulling the jar free from my hand.

Now this situation is similar, same but different. Same in the sense it's a tight fit to pull my one hand free, different in that I don't have the drunk person mindset, the one that thinks they are invincible. As I continue to wiggle and pull, I pray that traffic slows down again. He's almost completely clear of Main Street, and I need him to be slowed down enough to make a break for it. I bite down a frustrated groan and whisper-shout, "Come *on*," under my breath, the words slipping out sharper than I intend.

Realizing my mistake, I snap my gaze back to him, forcing a casual smile. Our eyes lock in the rearview mirror, and I see his brow crease like he caught me in action. My pulse picks up speed again, this time not from fear of being caught but from the intensity of his eyes. Those dark green irises pin me in place. For a moment, I almost forget he's my captor.

Clearing my throat and attempting to break free from his smoldering gaze, I resume my questioning.

"Are we there yet? I feel like we're not there yet. This is giving slow-burn angst."

He doesn't answer. Just keeps his eyes on the road, jaw tight.

"Wow," I say, leaning back and letting my voice drip with mock admiration. "You really go full grumpy silent type, huh?"

He flicks a quick glance, dark eyes narrowing, and grunts his response.

"Do all your sentences just come out in grunts, or is that just special treatment for me?"

"Do you ever stop talking?" His rich voice takes me by surprise.

"Oh my god, you speak! I was starting to think you were mute. This is huge character development for you!"

His hand tightens on the wheel. "Look, princess, we'll be there before you know it, so do us both a favor and quiet down back there."

"Princess?" I say, voice light and teasing. "Are we giving each other nicknames now? Is that what you call all your captives, or am I just special?"

He growls, low and almost amused. "The term fits you."

"Flattering," I shoot back. "What shall I call you? It's only fair we exchange terms of endearment."

"Terms of endearment?"

"Yes, you know the ones that're special to just us but will make others want to cringe."

I swear I see a smirk forming on the side of his face. For a moment, I forget I'm his captive and he's my captor. I almost forget all about my escape plan. That is, until my phone starts to vibrate against my thigh. My heart leaps. Yes. A lifeline! I start wiggling my hand faster, the rope giving all the way that I'm able to pull one hand free. A small burst of victory fills my chest. I quickly grab my phone, trying to get to the messages, hoping it's Clarie checking on me. I try to discreetly hide my phone and text, like I'm back in high school, hiding my phone from Mr. Ferguson in fifth-period Geometry.

I get as far as opening my home screen when a large hand grasps my wrist. I let out a startled yelp just as he snatches my phone out of my hand.

"Hey!" My entire world feels like it's ripped from my hand.

He doesn't respond, just tosses the phone into the console without looking back.

God damnit! Now what am I supposed to do?

My fingers curl into fists, nails biting into my palms, trying to anchor myself. I can feel the tears beginning to pool in my eyes. That was my only lifeline. I close my eyes, willing the tears not to fall. I am stronger than this. *I will* get through this.

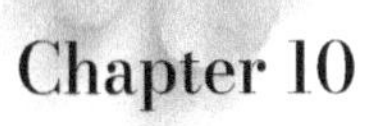

Chapter 10

Aiden

I can't believe I cracked. Talking to her is like feeding a raccoon—once you give it a snack, it never goes away. I don't even know why I called her *princess*. It was the first thing that came to my mind after seeing her walk along the street earlier. Full of grace and confidence.

This is bad. This is *really bad*. I can't seem to shake this weird energy she has on me. This is not happening. I'm not letting this delusional dark romance-loving chatterbox get under my skin.

SHE. IS. ELI'S. GIRL. FRIEND.

I repeat the mantra in my head, hoping it keeps me from doing something wrong, like continuing to drive her to a secluded cabin so we can spend the weekend getting to know each other. That's definitely what a sane person would do.

Rubbing my temple to alleviate this impending headache she has bestowed on me, I notice movement in my peripheral. Back when I served, I was always the one leading the mission. I had a sixth sense for things. I'm not exactly sure how I did it, but my peripheral sense was the best of the team. Trusting my gut, I turn around, and a mini heart attack hits me. She has a phone in her hand. A. PHONE. Where the fuck did she get the phone? Scared that she'll call the police, I quickly snatch it from her hands.

"Hey!" she protests.

Like that will get your phone back, princess.

Not a chance.

I pinch the bridge of my nose. I can practically feel the headache setting in. And then—the cherry on top—a police cruiser merges in front of my car. My soul leaves my body.

Sensing my rising panic, she leans forward and lets out a low hum.

"You know," she says, big doe eyes peeking up at me, "you could remove your mask. I mean, it would look less suspicious. Unless you want to be caught stuck in bumper-to-bumper traffic looking like you're about to rob a gas station."

"How did you get out of your restraints?" I ignore her taunt to remove my masks.

"Oh, this?" She's holding up the rope like it's a tangled shoelace she can't be bothered to deal with. There's no fear in her eyes, no hint of panic.

The corner of my mouth twitches before I can stop it. She should be trembling, begging, *something*. But instead, she's calm and collected. Either she's completely out of her mind, or she's got the kind of backbone most people spend their whole lives trying to fake. I know I didn't tie the rope as tight as I should have, but I wasn't trying to cut off her circulation. Still, this girl is impressive.

"This is nothing. You barely tightened the rope."

"Oh really," I say, amused at her bravado. "Have experience with getting out of rope restraints, princess?" My voice is low and a little more seductive than I intended. I catch her eyes in the rearview mirror; her glare doesn't hide the flicker of heat in her eyes, and the pink on her cheeks says she felt that just as much as I did.

"So," her voice is faint, a little awkward and hesitant, like she's unsure of her next steps. Honestly, so am I. She's untied and doesn't have her phone, but that still doesn't mean she won't try to fight me to get out.

"Why are you kidnapping me? I mean, it's not like I have any money. Or is it because of my beauty?"

I nearly choke on my next breath. "Yeah, that's it. I woke up this morning and thought... you know what sounds fun? Committing a felony for a pretty face."

She gasps in mock offense. "So you are saying I'm pretty."

"No. I did not say that."

"*Okay*, so is this like a side gig? The hospital doesn't pay you enough so you kidnap girls on the side?"

Shit. She must have spotted the badge before I hid it. Did she see my name or the hospital name? "I don't know what you mean."

"Right. What's your angle? Just tell me and maybe we can come to a mutual agreement."

A part of me is tempted.

This all can be over if I just tell her the plan Eli has and why I'm kidnapping her. I mean, logically, that's the right decision. Tell her to keep the secret, have her pretend like she doesn't know, and we can end this charade. But logic won't make for a good story to tell.

Chapter 11

Charlie

I'm so close to cracking him, I can feel it.

The traffic has opened up completely, and we're crashing down Main Street at a good pace. I could pull a James Bond move, unlock the car, and roll out. I am contemplating my next move when my bladder is staging a full-blown protest, those two cups of coffee hitting me at full force. Each bump in the road has it screaming at me like an angry toddler denied a toy at Target. If we don't stop soon, I might end up peeing my pants. How humiliating would that be? Tied up in the back seat of my captor's car. Wet. And not the fun kind.

"Uh, so," I shift in the seat, crossing and uncrossing my legs. "Quick question. How... How far are we going?" I can feel the building tingly sensation running up my spine. I'm about to explode.

His eyes flick from the road to me, lifting one brow. "Why?"

"Because I really, really need to use the little girl's room," I admit, cheeks heated from my admission. "Like, code red level, we need to pull over *right now*." Panic laces my voice.

He must sense my distress, or he's a really nice captor. Or

maybe he just doesn't want me to get his car dirty. Probably that option. What captor would care about the random girl in his back seat? He starts to signal to turn right at the upcoming street.

A familiar street sign comes into view: Maple Lane. As I expected, we've barely made it anywhere. We only made it to the end of Main Street. Maple Lane is the quietest and coziest street in Everly Falls. In contrast to the hustle and bustle of Main Street, Maple Lane is lined with low storefronts and sleepy sidewalks. A few mom-and-pop businesses line the street. Maple Diner is among them, a staple of our little town, and the perfect location to stop.

It is *the* place to be after the high school football game wraps up. Dee Dee and Pop, the owners, are basically honorary parents to every one of us. If I can convince him to stop, I know Dee Dee will help me. She'll take one look at this out-of-towner, give me a wink, and send me out the back door with her famous peach cobbler while Pop sequesters him and calls the sheriff.

"We need to stop at the first location you see." Knowing the first business down this street is Maple Diner, there's no way he can avoid it.

His eyes narrow. "You've got to be kidding me."

"Nope." I shake my head excessively, hoping he will take pity on me.

"This ship is sinking. The Titanic has hit the iceberg, Captain."

Groaning under his breath, he mutters something that sounds suspiciously like *why me?*

"Look, there's a little diner up ahead," I say, nodding toward the billboard along the side of the road. The weathered sign with chipped paint and a faded red maple leaf barely cling to the wood. *Maple Diner. Best peach cobbler in Everly Falls.*

The sign's so worn it's almost a landmark. All the tourists

stop there because they're told to, every local has a favorite booth with the cracked vinyl, and no one leaves without a serving of Dee Dee's famous peach cobbler. That cobbler has won more blue ribbons at the annual Farmer's Market than I can count.

I can sense his glare even if he isn't looking at me. At this point, I would promise not to ask anyone for help if he agreed to stop right away. I'm hanging on by a thread. Taking advantage of the stoplight, I lean forward and touch his biceps—the touch is light yet electrifying.

"Look," I start, executing the best puppy dog eyes I have ever performed—like showman worthy, I could win a blue ribbon for these eyes. "I promise to be on my best behavior and not try to escape or ask anyone for help, if we can just stop at the diner for the little girl's room."

"Alright, but you need to be quick," he relents.

"Thank you," I say, genuinely thankful for him agreeing.

The parking lot is scarce with cars, likely because everyone is gathering on Main Street. *Damn it.* I know I promised not to run away, but that did not mean I wasn't going to try to slip the service staff a note. It might be harder to do with fewer patrons to distract him.

He gets out from his side of the car and, in an instant, he opens my door, his body blocking my escape. He is massive, taking up the entire opening of the door. He looks sturdy, too; it would take a lot of effort for me to push him out of the way and run.

He leans in close, closer than I'm expecting. I catch a whiff of him again, smoke and cedar—it's intoxicating in such close proximity. Without my mind's consent, I close my eyes and take a deep inhale. He clears his throat, and my eyes fly open to find a smirk on his face, heat creeping up my neck from embarrassment.

"Remember, princess, no funny business."

Before I can say anything, he takes my hand and leads me toward the diner. My body feels like a live wire with his close proximity. Hand in hand, we look like a couple out on a brunch date.

The bell to the diner chimes as we walk inside. Stepping in, a wave of nostalgia hits me. The diner still has its original charm. Rows of red leather booths line the sides, their vinyl cushions slightly cracked but still full of charm. The floor has the original black-and-white checkered floor. The smell of frying bacon, fresh coffee, and butter sizzling on the griddle hits my senses, making me forget why we were here in the first place.

"How many?" a perky waitress says, walking our way. She looks too pretty to be working at the diner. She reminds me of my friend Jade, a striking elegance of a runway model and legs that go on for days. At five-four, I was always a little jealous of her height. When she wore bell-bottom jeans, she looked like she'd just stepped off a runway. Meanwhile, I looked like Humpty Dumpty who stepped off the wall.

"Actually, where's your restroom?" I blurt out, shifting on my feet, really feeling the push on my bladder now that I am standing still.

"Oh, the second door on the right," she replies, not meeting my eye and blatantly staring at my captor. I'm not going to lie, he does look insanely attractive with that skeleton neck gaiter covering half his face. Like he walked straight out of a dark romance novel. His emerald eyes are on full display, and dark curls of his hair look soft and touchable, but that doesn't give her the right to ogle him with me standing right here. A surge of unwelcome jealousy washes over me. I don't know why, it's not like I'm dating him. I really need to refocus on the fact that I'm here against my free will and not excited to be getting breakfast with this tall and broody guy.

"I'll be right over there." My captor points to the closest booth to the restroom hallway.

I rush off like my pants are on fire. I need to relieve myself like a toddler after three boxes of apple juice. I make my way down the hallway toward the single person restroom. As soon as my butt hits the seat, my heart sinks. OH MY GOD, the universe hates me. What kind of bad karma did I accumulate over the course of my life that my body chose today, *of all days*, to start my menstrual cycle? Of everything that is already happening today, I think this one takes the cake.

I glance around the small restroom hoping to find any kind of feminine product I can use. I check the small cabinet next to the toilet, praying for something. *Nothing*. I'm in full panic mode when I hear a knock on the door, and an annoying grumpy voice floats through the door.

"Hey! Are you done in there? We have to go."

"Umm..." I sound more timid than I expect, "I have a situation."

"What situation?" His voice is hesitant, like he's unsure what new chaos I'm about to unleash on him. *Oh, you're in it now, Mr. Man.*

"Could you maybe ask the waitress to come to the door?"

"No. Tell me what it is."

"Well, I started my cycle, there isn't any feminine product in here, and I can't leave. It's like Shark Week in here." I wince as soon as that analogy leaves my mouth. *He didn't need to know that, Charlie.*

No response, just sounds of footsteps walking away. I would have left, too, because that was embarrassing. It feels like an eternity passes as I sit in the small restroom, thinking of my next move.

A knock rattles the flimsy restroom door, and I nearly jump out of my skin. His voice carries through a second later, low but surprisingly sympathetic.

"The waitress didn't have anything on hand, so I'm heading next door to the convenience store to get you what you need. Don't try anything funny."

I'm too stunned to reply. He's really going to buy me feminine products? Most guys would die of embarrassment just walking down that aisle. Before I can even get a word out, his footsteps are already retreating.

Chapter 12

Aiden

Sliding into the vinyl booth, I sink back against the squeaky red cushion and let my eyes sweep over the place. This diner looks like it stepped out of the 70s—linoleum floors scuffed from years of boots and sneakers, a jukebox in the corner covered in faded stickers, and laminated menus tucked between salt and pepper shakers.

Alone for the first time, I tug the gaiter down to get some fresh air. It reeks of sweat and bad decisions like every boy ski trip I've taken. The last time I wore this mask, we were racing down a black run at Copper Mountain when our classmate, Luke, wiped out and popped his shoulder clean out of the socket. Good thing Eli was training in sports medicine—he'd seen his fair share of dislocations. He got Luke patched up and down the mountain for treatment like it was just another Tuesday.

I scratch my beard while examining the menu. I could use a little breakfast, but I doubt we have the time. Eli said to meet at noon. Traffic has already delayed us and it's not a quarter past ten.

"Would you like a cup of coffee?" the waitress's voice interrupts my thought. She's leaning her right hip against the booth, puffing out her chest, definitely trying to flirt, but my focus is on the brunette in the restroom.

I shake my head, eyes flicking toward the restroom door for the third time in the last minute. She's been in there too long. My gut twists—did she run off? I'm sitting at the entrance of the hallway. She couldn't have made it past me. But what if there's a back door next to the restroom? I curse myself for not checking before letting her go in alone. A rush of fear sweeps over me as I think about the blaring police cruiser that's about to show up outside the dinner. But another emotion is clogging at my throat, a low hum of worry I can't quite shake. Worry for *her* safety.

I walk toward the restroom, praying she has not slipped out the back door. Spotting no viable exit in sight, I knock on the restroom door to check on her.

"Hey! Are you done there? We have to go." My voice is harsher than I intend.

"Umm..." her meek voice floats through the door, "I have a situation."

Instantly, I'm on high alert.

"What situation?" I ask, trying to sound as calm as I can, even with my insides telling me I need to break this door down and protect her from all her demons.

"Could you maybe ask the waitress to come to the door?"

"No. Tell me what it is." My mind is running a mile a minute at her deflection.

"Well, I started my cycle, there isn't any feminine product in here, and I can't leave. It's like Shark Week in here."

It takes a full minute for what she said to sink in, and then I'm off. In full situational control mode. I know firsthand what this is like—having a little sister will do that to you. I remember it like it was yesterday, when my baby sister, Ava, got her first cycle. Without our mom, Ava grew up without that steady female figure to guide her through the awkward years. My dad was incredible, and together we did our best, but some things require a softer, more feminine touch. Thank goodness for my Aunt Maeve. She made sure Ava had someone to talk to, someone to teach her the things we couldn't.

Still, when it came to the day-to-day emotional storms and hormonal roller coasters of Ava's teenage years, I became the stand-in expert. We were five years apart, and I made it my mission to always have her back. If that meant the occasional late-night run to the store for tampons and a Snickers bar, then that's exactly what I did.

Making my way to the hostess stand, I spot the waitress. Not wasting a minute on pleasantries, I get right to the point.

"Do you have any spare feminine products?"

Her brows shoot up. "Umm, I don't know. I can check." Confusion flickers across her face; she's probably not used to a guy asking her that, let alone one who's six-four and covered in ink.

She disappears for a moment and comes back shaking her head. "Sorry, no luck. There's a convenience store two shops down. They should have something."

I nod once, already shifting into motion. No hesitation. I rush back toward the restroom to let her know I'm heading out to grab what she needs.

"The waitress didn't have anything on hand, so I'm heading next door to the convenience store to get you what you need." I start to turn around, but then remember I'm technically her captor, so I add, "Don't try anything funny."

* * *

The bell above the glass door jingles as I push through the front door. The place is quaint, just what you would expect from a small town. Rows of narrow aisles stretch out in front of me—chips and candy bars stacked in neat chaos, soda bottles sweating in refrigerated coolers along the back wall.

It takes me a second to scan the personal care aisle—razors, toothpaste, travel-size deodorant—before I find the shelf I'm looking for. Does she prefer pads over tampons? Does she like the pads with wings or without wings? Without hesitating, I grab one of everything since I don't know what she prefers.

My arms are full, and I don't care if I look ridiculous as I make my way to the front checkout. An older man stands behind the counter. He looks a little like Santa Claus with his round belly and a full gray beard, but his eyes are sharp, bright, almost mischievous.

"You got the whole store here," he says, his voice gravelly but warm as he scans the boxes of tampons and pads, dropping them into a paper sack. His lips twitch, fighting a grin.

"Yeah, I guess so," I say casually, shifting the armful onto the counter.

He chuckles, the sound low and knowing. "She must be someone special. Back in my day, a man only braved this aisle if he was married. Or desperate."

"It's, uh, not like that." I clear my throat, scanning the impulse-buy items. I spot the Snickers bars, sliding two in with the rest of my items.

His eyebrows lift, his beard twitching with the beginnings of a smile. "She could use someone in her corner. You take care of her now."

Before I can get him to elaborate, he pushes the paper bag toward me and waves a hand at the door.

Puzzled, I make my way back to the diner.

* * *

Placing a gentle knock on the door to not startle her, I ask, "You good in there?"

"Not really," she says, her voice sounding defeated and tired. "This is *so* embarrassing."

"Nothing to be embarrassed about. Normal biological function. I got you what you need. I'll just leave it here at the door, and I'll be at the booth when you're ready." Setting the bag down gently, I turn to walk away without another word, giving her the space she needs.

Chapter 13

Charlie

There are only a few moments in my life I'd call truly embarrassing. Like the time I got my front teeth knocked out playing tetherball when I was eight, or the time my skirt got stuck on the escalator and I had to wait for the fire department to untangle me. This moment? Beats them all.

A soft knock breaks me from my self-pity. My captor's voice comes through the door. "You good in there?" His voice is gentle, not at all judgmental.

"Not really." I let out a long exhale, defeated and tired. "This is *so* embarrassing."

"Nothing to be embarrassed about. Normal biological function. I got you what you need. I'll just leave it here at the door, and I'll be at the booth when you're ready." The reassuring words and his calmness soothe me.

I hear footsteps receding. Wrapping a handful of toilet paper around my hand to make a makeshift pad, I slide it into place and adjust so I can make my way to the door.

I gasp when I open the bag. There's a plethora of feminine

products—like he bought the entire aisle. Smiling to myself, I grab what I need and get myself situated.

After what feels like an hour trapped in this restroom, I'm ready to leave. I wash my hands, grab the bag, and stop when I notice two Snickers bars at the bottom. How did he know my favorite candy?

Thoughts of this captor swirl in my head. Maybe he's someone I know? Maybe this isn't really a kidnapping at all?

Making my way back to the front, I scan the small diner looking for my captor when my breath catches in my throat. He must have taken his mask and hoodie off while I was in the restroom. He looks more relaxed, at ease even. He doesn't appear to be a captor. At this moment, he looks like he belongs in this small town.

I know I am shamelessly checking him out but I cannot help it. His full face is on display—and wow, it's a good-looking face. Sharp jawline, full beard, but not the rugged mountain beard. He looks well-groomed, like he took the time to take care of it. High cheekbones that catch the light, making his eyes stand out even more—deep, dark, and unreadable, like he's hiding a secret just for me. His lips are full, the kind that make you think they're meant for mischief, or maybe a kiss. And his messy curly black hair makes me want to run my fingers through it. I'm transfixed on his forearm—tattoos snake up his skin, black lines twisting over his bicep muscle and disappearing under his shirt. My gaze follows the ink trail up to his neck, where intricate designs peek out beneath the collar. Heat prickles my chest and neck before I even realize it. This is it. My instant-attraction trope in real time.

His eyes catch mine, and I give a sheepish smile, mortified that he caught me staring. Reeling my hormones back into my body and letting my brain take control again, I make my way over to the booth.

"Thanks for buying the whole store," I joke, sliding into the booth opposite him.

His lips twitch up in a small smirk, and I find myself wondering what he would look like with a full smile.

"Don't mention it. I have experience with this. I know how rough this time of the month can be."

I wonder how he's had experience. Does he have a girlfriend? The thought slips in before I can stop it, and jealousy rolls through me for the second time today, hot and irrational.

He must see the look on my face, because he chuckles, low and warm, the sound vibrating between us. He leans back in the booth, one arm draping casually across the top like he owns the space.

"I have a little sister," he explains, eyes softening as he remembers their relationship. "Trust me, I've seen it all. Did you find the chocolate? She used to swear up and down that chocolate could cure anything."

"Yes, I did find it." I can't stop the little smile tugging at my lips. He's kind of sweet, in a tatted, broad-shouldered, kinda way. I toy with the wrapper between my fingers, letting the crinkle fill the silence. "How did you know Snickers were my favorite?"

"Lucky guess." His mouth tips into a half smile, dimples threatening to appear. My god, this man has dimples? My poor ovaries are ready to go to any secluded cabins he has in mind.

I must be staring too long because his brows draw together, a puzzled look across his face.

"What?" His voice dips low with confusion.

I swallow, my fingers playing with the wrapper of the candy bar. I didn't need to melt into a puddle of mush from the intensity of his eyes. Steadying my breath to remain as nonchalant as I can, I muster up one sentence. "You look good without your mask."

Chapter 14

Aiden

My eyes widen because, somewhere between all this chaos, I had forgotten about my mask. I begin to formulate some excuse for this kidnapping ruse when I catch her eyes trail over me in a slow sweep. She's checking me out. A rush of pride courses through me. Without realizing, I straighten and push out my chest.

"You done staring, or should I give you a twirl?" I tease, loving the way her cheeks flush.

"I wasn't staring," she backpedals. "You look different than I expected."

"Different good?" I lean in, smirking. I must be a glutton for punishment, flirting with my best friend's girl.

She fiddles with the straw in her water glass, avoiding my gaze. "Let's just say if our trope went from captor to lover, I would not be mad."

My mind starts racing. She's definitely flirting back—and if that's the case, maybe she's not as good for Eli as he thinks. This mission just shifted from a kidnapping to a full-on covert operation. I'm going to expose her for who she really is.

I let out a low chuckle, the sound making her glance up. "Careful, princess. Sounds like you're flirting."

The sound of her stomach breaks our conversation.

"Oh my god, this day could not get any worse," she says, covering her face with both her hands.

"Are you hungry? We can get some food." I don't know why I'm offering to sit down and have a meal with her when I should really be getting her to Eli. Part of me doesn't want this morning to end.

"You're feeding your hostage? That feels very 'Stockholm syndrome starter pack' of you," she quips, making me roll my eyes.

Before I can retort, she lets out an exhausted sigh, fingers fidgeting with the sleeves of her sweater, making her look small and vulnerable. "That actually sounds perfect. I could really go for a hot cocoa and, like, ten pancakes." The morning toll must have finally caught up with her. A faint ache blooms in my chest, a mix of guilt and the strange urge to make it up to her somehow.

We place our order and a mug of hot cocoa, with an ungodly amount of whipped cream, appears less than a second later. Like they had fully anticipated her order.

"So," she says, taking a sip of her hot cocoa and leveling me with a look that makes me want to spill everything about myself, "do you want to play twenty questions?"

I grin. "You want to play twenty questions? Like speed dating?"

"Yup!" She pops the *P* in all seriousness.

"You want to date me, princess?"

I catch the way she shifts in her seat, gaze flicking anywhere but me.

She's flustered. That's cute. "Alright, rapid-fire or the soul-searching kind?"

"Rapid-fire," she says, tapping the edge of her mug.

"Fine. But if any of this gets too annoying, I swear—"

"First question!" she starts, pointing a finger like she's a game show host. "Favorite color?"

"Black." Her hand flies up to cover her mouth as a chuckle leaves her lips, the sound cute and endearing.

"What?"

"You're wearing all black right now," she teases, holding back another chuckle.

"Okay, fine, your turn?"

"Pink, obviously." She gestures at her sweater, which has slipped off her shoulder again, giving me another peek of her collarbone. The olive color is like a beacon calling me home; I want to nestle my nose into the crook of her neck.

Clearing my throat, I try not to think about how soft her skin would feel under me. "Next question."

"Favorite food?"

"Steak. Rare."

"Ewww. Like with the blood running out of it?" Her nose wrinkles like she just ate something sour. It's incredibly charming.

"Yeah," I say, smirking. "That's how you know it's actually good. What about you?"

"Green bean casserole. I know, I know, it's a holiday dish, but I love it so much I could probably eat it daily." She can not be more adorable; she's giving Jake a run for his money.

"Favorite guilty pleasure?" she presses on.

"Cheesy rom-coms. And I'm not ashamed."

She laughs, and the sound hits me in a way I can't ignore. "Of course you aren't. What movie?"

"*She's the Man*," I say, watching her eyes light up.

"Shut up! You're lying, that's my favorite movie!" She's bouncing in her seat with giddiness.

Proving that it is indeed her favorite movie, she begins

imitating the famous lines. "'Do you like cheese? Why yes, my favorite is Gouda.'"

I can't help but laugh along with her. Something about her just eases my tension and makes me feel weightless. All the stress from residency applications, my rotation, my responsibility for Jake, and even this kidnapping—it all evaporates the longer I sit here talking to her.

She tucks one of the hairs falling around her face behind her ear, the movement causing a faint scent of vanilla to waft over me. Her eyes sparkle when she smiles, and I swear my chest tightens every time they meet mine. I shouldn't have noticed her smile. I shouldn't care. But I do. And I can't stop myself. We stop talking as the waitress drops off our food. She was not kidding when she said she wanted ten pancakes; the stack is so tall it almost comes up to her chin. I'm not even sure where she's going to fit them all.

I ordered the Pops' Special from the menu: two eggs, crispy bacon, and a warm, flaky homemade biscuit. My mouth waters and stomach rumbles before I even pick up my fork. I didn't have breakfast this morning since I was trying to get to her in time.

"Okay, what about a dream vacation?" She glances up at me while spreading butter on every single one of her pancakes, her long lashes framing her doe brown eyes. As a physician, I am genuinely worried about her cholesterol health. That's a lot of butter.

"Somewhere cold and secluded, like the mountains. You?"

"Definitely a beach, toes in the sand, and a good book in my hand. The perfect vacation."

Instantly, I'm picturing her on the beach in a dark green bikini, the color complementing her olive-toned skin and bringing out the color of her eyes. I shouldn't be thinking of her this way but can't seem to stop myself when it comes to her. Every time she fires off another question, it's like she reels me in a little tighter, her grin daring me to play along.

Chapter 15

Charlie

Maybe I've hit my head on the island counter one too many times while baking, but I swear, I'm having *fun* getting to know my captor. Which is absolutely insane. Who enjoys a kidnapping? Yet here I am, sitting across from him, laughing like this is some twisted first date instead of a felony in progress.

I'm still slightly worried this kidnapping might be the real deal, but a small, delusional part of me is holding out hope for a captor-to-lovers story arc. Because honestly? He's making it hard to remember I'm supposed to be terrified. The man brought me an entire store's worth of feminine products and chocolate, and is currently feeding me enough carbs to feed a small village. It's like he graduated top of his class in Book Boyfriend 101.

And I swear he's flirting with me. Or maybe I'm just projecting. Still, I really hope he is flirting because if he's into me, maybe he'll reconsider killing me.

"Y'all doing okay over here?" Dee Dee's voice startles me from my thoughts. She smiles as she tips the pot of fresh coffee toward his half-empty cup.

Her silver-streaked waves sway as she leans in, catching the morning sun streaming through the blinds. The floral perfume she always wears wraps around me, familiar but a tad suffocating. Like did she spritz or douse in it this morning?

Looking into her blue eyes, I remember why I insisted on coming here. I knew this was it. The moment I've been waiting for to escape. All I need to do is subtly send her a signal, something inconspicuous. But before I can open my mouth, her eyes flick from him to me, and her smile widens. A mischievous grin spread across her face. Oh shit. I know that face. She thinks we're on a date.

"Well, hi there, sugarplum. Who's your friend?"

Of course, the town matchmaker is more worried about hitching up us poor single souls than recognizing a kidnapping when she sees one. Dee Dee's famous for her match-making skills—rumor has it she can size up a couple in thirty seconds flat and declare them a perfect match. People actually come from out of town to get her seal of approval before their weddings. More than once, a teary-eyed fiancé has come running out of the diner after getting the bad news.

And to be fair, without the sack over my head, the bound wrists, or his mask, we look like the picture-perfect date. The kind you'd scroll past on Instagram with a heart emoji and a "couple goals" comment—minus the felony.

"Oh, this is…uh—" What was I supposed to say? This is my captor, name redacted because I still don't know if he's going to kill me or not.

"I'm Aiden," he interjects, like we're networking at some business mixer.

Aiden. The name suits him. I know it's Celtic—something about fire and nature. You read one dark romance book about a Celtic warlord and end up three hours deep into a name-meaning rabbit hole. Apparently, "Aiden" means "little fire." Which tracks, because we're in that slow-burn trope, and he's exuding that *ruin me in the best way* kind of energy.

"Nice to meet you!" Dee Dee beams. "Don't let me interrupt. I know a first date when I see one." She looks at me conspiratorially.

I nearly choke on my hot cocoa, sputtering against the whipped cream. You're boyfriendless for three years, and suddenly every guy you are with is your date.

"Don't be shy," she says with a wink, her smile crinkling the corners of her eyes. "I've got an eye for these things, and I haven't seen you smile like that in a long time."

My cheeks flame, the heat prickling my skin. I shake my head so fast I'm worried I might get whiplash. "It's not like that."

Aiden clears his throat, probably trying to get Dee Dee to leave so he can get on with this kidnapping. I'm positive the previous girls he kidnapped weren't this embarrassing. A wave of possessiveness courses through me at the thought of him with other captives. How illogical, considering they're probably dead because of him. But something about his eyes doesn't scream *I'm a killer!*

"We're not on a date." His definitive tone leaves no room for argument.

Well, that's a blow to the ego. Not that I expected us to be on a date. Just because he's the first nice guy I've been around in years doesn't make him my potential date.

"Mmhmm. Sure, you aren't. I know a first date when I see one." She scribbles something onto her pad, probably adding my name to her ever-growing mental matchmaking list.

"Don't mess it up, handsome. Trust me, this girl's a keeper."

My fingers toy nervously with the rim of my cup. "Well, that was Dee Dee. She's the owner of this diner. She and Pop have been running this place for as long as I can remember.

She's a little bit much." I chuckle, thinking back to all the times Claire and I sat in this diner talking about boys. I wonder if I'll be back here with her soon, talking about my captor. The captor, who is turning out to be a sweet softie, versus his kidnapping intention. Even though logic is telling me this is dangerous, something deep inside me is saying he's safe, he's steady, and I can trust him.

Chapter 16

Aiden

D ee Dee's words hang in the air. "Don't mess it up, handsome. Trust me, this girl's a keeper." Her sneakers squeak against the linoleum as she moves to the next booth.

It has been so easy sitting here chatting with her, forgetting what I'm actually supposed to be doing—exposing her true nature. Our conversation flows so effortlessly, no strain or awkward silences. She's relaxed, like she's in her natural element, as she fires question after question at me. There's this calm air between us; it makes me want to share all my secrets, every unpolished thought I usually keep locked away. A companionship I didn't realize I had been missing, craving, until now.

"Do you have any pets?" She resumes her questioning between bites of her pancakes.

"Yeah," I mutter casually, though my lips twitch despite myself. "His name's Jake."

Her brows lift, eyes narrowing as though she's about to pounce. "Dog or cat?"

"Dog," I answer, my smirk breaking free as I think about my mischievous canine companion.

"Jake?" she repeats, like it's a revelation. "That's a very human name for a dog. Aren't dogs supposed to have cute nicknames like Biscuit, Waffles, or Sparky?" she teases. She doesn't seem to notice that she's leaning in closer, and without my brain's consent, my own body leans in, too.

I smirk. "He was originally named Butterscotch, but I wasn't going to be calling him that."

The sound of her giggle hits somewhere deep, catching me off guard. It's soft, breathy, and for some reason, my body reacts before my brain catches up. Thank god for the table between us.

"Yeah, I can't see a guy like you walking around the park saying 'Butterscotch.'"

My curiosity gets the better of me before I can stop it. "A guy like me? What kind of guy is that?"

She freezes. Just for a second. She's staring at her pancakes like they're going to sprout legs and walk away, her teeth catching her bottom lip like she regrets letting something slip. For the first time since she's been in my car, she seems almost shy. Interesting.

"Oh, you know," she says, fidgeting, "big, broody, built like he could lift a car—but probably apologizes when he bumps into people."

I bite back a laugh. "Lift a car?"

She winces, shy and awkward, like the second those words left her mouth, she wished she could pull them back. "I mean, you just have that look," she adds quickly, cheeks flushing pink. "Not that I think about you lifting cars or bumping into people. Or at all, really."

Her rambling is pure entertainment, and I can't stop the smile that tugs at the corner of my mouth.

"Right," I say, leaning back just enough to watch her squirm. "Definitely not thinking about me."

Her lips press together, and she hides behind her cup like it's a shield. "Glad we're on the same page," she mumbles.

She's cute when she's flustered. The kind of cute that makes my brain short-circuit and my chest feel too tight. I should look away, stop staring, stop noticing how her hair falls forward when she ducks her head or how the corner of her mouth curves when she's trying not to smile. But I don't.

Instead, I take a slow sip of coffee and let the moment stretch.

Her eyes flick up to meet mine, just for a second, and something in my chest gives a traitorous lurch.

I'm so screwed.

Because this isn't supposed to be happening. I shouldn't care if she blushes or fumbles over her words. I shouldn't want to keep her talking just to see how many shades of pink her cheeks can turn. But here I am, sitting across from her, fighting a losing battle against a smile that refuses to die.

"What kind of dog do you have?" she asks quickly, clearly desperate to change the subject.

"A Maltese-Yorkie mix. He's about a year old, full of energy. Steals any socks he can get his paws on. He would eat peanut butter straight from the jar if I let him."

"Wait, he eats peanut butter straight from the jar?" she asks, eyes wide with fascination. "That's impressive, but isn't it dangerous?"

"Not really," I say, remembering the amount of peanut butter jars I have purchased from Costco. "I trained him to wait for it. Mostly. Sometimes he cheats. He's stubborn and super manipulative but fiercely loyal."

"Sounds like a handful. I wish I had a dog. I just don't have the time right now."

"Why don't you have time?" I understand why I'm asking

more personable questions but this insatiable need to know more about her is clawing out.

"The microbakery is so much work, I barely have time to take care of myself, let alone another living thing."

At her confession, I let myself take a closer look, and it hits me how exhausted she appears. Dark circles shadow the corners of her eyes, faint lines crease her forehead, and her shoulders slump just slightly. My chest tightens at the thought that she's been running on empty this whole time.

My brain latches on to her job. She's a baker, but I thought Eli said his girlfriend was a photographer. Where would she find the time? Is she lying about being a photographer, maybe to go and meet other guys? Like what she's trying to do here, have her cake and eat it, too.

Before I can dwell on that thought, her next question catches me off guard.

"Can I meet him?"

I stiffen. "Umm, sure, maybe someday," I say carefully.

She groans in mock exasperation. "Fine. But that day better come soon, mister broody captor. Jake sounds like such a good boy."

Her voice drops into a sultry tone when she says good boy. A shiver runs through me, a sudden jolt of awareness I can't entirely explain, and heat blooms over every inch of my body.

"So," she says, taking a sip of her cocoa, "you have a sister?"

"Yeah," I say, thinking of Ava and what she's up to in North Carolina, "her name is Ava."

"Is she older than you?"

"No, she's five years younger than me."

"How old are you?" she asks with a hint of curiosity.

"I'm thirty-four. Why? Is that a problem?" I smirk at the way she fidgets with the sleeves of her sweater. I've noticed she does that whenever she's shy or nervous about the situation. I notice a lot of things about her—that I shouldn't be noticing.

"No. Not a problem. I'm twenty-six so that's actually perfect. Age-gap trope is my favorite," she says, winking at me. I swear my heart skips a beat.

"How did you become the designated feminine product fetcher?" she continues, not realizing the effect she has on me.

"Our mom passed away when Ava was born, and she didn't have a female figure growing up. It was the least I could do. Late-night purchases for tampons and chocolate were my specialty." I'm not sure why I'm sharing all this information with her, except that I want to. There's something warm and inviting about her that makes me want to share all my secrets.

"I'm so sorry." Her voice is soft and comforting. No pity in her tone, like others when I've shared my past, just genuine compassion.

"Thanks," I manage to say, trying to keep from swallowing against the tightness in my throat. I look down at my coffee cup, swirling the liquid, keeping my hands busy. "It was a long time ago, and I barely have any memories of her. It's worse for Ava. She didn't have any memories growing up."

She nods slowly. "That must have been tough."

I glance up, caught by the sincerity in her expression. For a second, the noise of the cafe fades and it's just us, suspended in this bubble that is all ours.

As if the universe has impeccable comedic timing, my phone lights up with Eli's name. My stomach drops. I need to act casual, like I'm not sitting here trying to catfish his girlfriend into revealing her true nature so he can move on to a better girl.

Eli's voice rings through my phone, slightly breathless—like he's been running a marathon. "Hey, dude, we have to abort the mission. Claire is freaking out that her sister's missing. I need to meet her at the bookstore before she has a full-on panic attack."

It takes a full sixty seconds for my brain to compute. His words hit one at a time, each heavier than the last.

Claire. Is. Freaking. Out.

Claire. Is. At. The. Bookstore.

Which means Claire is not sitting across from me, eating her Mount Everest-sized pancake tower.

My stomach sinks to the bottom of my feet. I can feel the color drain from my face. My mind replays the day. All I can focus on is the impending flashing red and blue lights heading toward the dinner, handcuffs digging into my wrists, and the potential of meeting my cellmate named Bubba.

"Dude, are you listening?" Eli's voice brings me back to the present. "I'm going to take Jake with me and meet Claire on Main Street. Her parents are joining so we can do a search of the area."

"Okay," my voice is husky, "I will meet you there." I hear rustling in the background. He must be leashing Jake to leave the house.

I hang up the phone, blinking at the girl across from me, my mouth dry, no words coming to my mind. How do I even begin to explain to this girl—who is not Claire, not Eli's girlfriend—a complete stranger, that I was kidnapping her for an immersive role play?

For a moment, the realization of her not being Eli's girlfriend hits me, quick and sharp. Thank god I haven't been lusting after my best friend's girlfriend. That thought vanishes just as fast, replaced by something far worse—dread. Pure, bone-deep dread. Because now? Now I *am* a kidnapper.

Yup, straight to jail.

Chapter 17

Charlie

If you had told me this morning I would be sitting at Maple Diner with my captor, enjoying our breakfast date, I would have told you you were crazy. Our conversation has been flowing non-stop. I've learned that he has a sister, a dog named Jake, shares the same favorite movie as me, is a fan of all holiday-flavored drinks, and a closet cinnamon roll. That last one is more of an observation than something he shared.

Our conversation ends abruptly when his phone vibrates. Pretending not to eavesdrop, I continue cutting into my pancake tower, dragging the fluffy piece through a puddle of maple syrup. The butter melts across my tongue, soft and sweet with just the right hint of salt. I know it's weird, but I don't like my pancakes drowned in syrup—they get too soggy. I'd rather dip as I go, controlling the texture of each bite.

Sensing his eyes on me, I glance up. He stops talking mid-sentence, his face pale and his eyebrows furrowing. My internal panic meter spikes, alarms blaring, reminding me this is not a first date but in fact a kidnapping. Fully aware I am overanalyzing his expression, but I can't help the rising panic.

What's with that look? Did someone just tell him I'm no longer useful? Is it time to *get rid* of me?

I break eye contact, darting a glance around the diner, desperate for the waitress, or Dee Dee, to swoop in and save me. My hand won't stop trembling, so I shove it under my thigh, pressing it hard against the sticky vinyl seat to keep it still. My pulse is in my throat, each beat louder than the clink of silverware and hum of conversation around us. I need to get the hell out of here. *Now.*

Before I can move, he leans forward, voice low. "I'm sorry," he says, running a hand through his curls. His voice entrances me for a second before it seeps in. Did he just apologize? For kidnapping me?

"I didn't... It wasn't supposed to be you," he continues, words tumbling out before he can form a full sentence. His eyes are guilty, almost haunted, and my stomach drops. What the hell does that even mean? *Wasn't supposed to be me?*

My pulse spikes, my hands trembling under the table. I don't know what's happening, and honestly, I don't think I want to. I just want to get out of here and back to my sister.

My eyes dart around the diner, desperate for someone to meet my gaze. To save me from whatever this is. The waitress passes by without so much as a glance, the couple in the corner too wrapped up in their breakfast to notice the girl silently pleading for help.

I could slide out of this booth so easily. Just stand up, walk away. I should've done it the second I realized he wasn't going to stop me. But instead, here I am—caught in his gravity. The kind of pull that shouldn't exist between captor and captive. All because he had the audacity to be nice and sound like my favorite audiobook narrator.

His next sentence cuts clean through the chaos in my head, quieting every frantic thought in an instant.

"God, Eli and his stupid ideas," he mutters under his breath.

My thoughts stutter and rewind. Did he just say Eli?

I stare at him, unblinking, heart hammering so loud I'm sure he can hear it. "Wait, did you just say Eli?" My voice comes out shakier than intended.

His jaw tightens, the muscle ticking like a warning, and he doesn't answer. Silence stretches between us, and every second makes my pulse spike higher.

"As in my sister's boyfriend, Eli?" I force the words out, my chest tightening with a mix of fury and disbelief.

Claire may be older by technicality, and she acts like the responsible older sister sometimes, but when it comes to her safety? I'm a mama bear. If this guy knows Eli, I need to get Claire away from them. I thought I had vetted Eli thoroughly, cross-checked every social profile, and dug into every little detail. Apparently, I missed something.

I remember the first time Claire told me she was going on a date with a guy she met at the charity flag football fundraiser. I'd spent all of five minutes listening before my brain kicked into full detective mode. Social media profiles, LinkedIn pages, old news articles, even a few random mentions on hospital forums—I knew everything. The FBI had nothing on me.

When Eli came to pick Claire up for their date, I went into full 007 mode. While she was finishing up getting ready, I cornered him in the living room—or, well, more like subtly interrogated him without looking suspicious. By the time Claire came out of her room, I already had a mental file on him—hometown, family, his favorite coffee.

My captor is staring at me, trying to assess what I know, at the same time I'm trying to assess him.

"How do you know Eli?"

Chapter 18

Aiden

I must be hallucinating from the stress. Did she just say her *sister*? Claire is her sister.

I try to rack my memory, sifting through every conversation I've had with Eli. Did he ever mention Claire having a sister? No. He said twin. A twin named Charlie. Like Charlie Brown, except clearly not, because sitting across from me is Claire's twin, who is definitely not a guy.

"You're Claire's sister?" I can't seem to comprehend this turn of events.

She stares at me like I've grown two heads. Her eyes narrow, sharp and cutting. "What are you talking about? Yes, I'm Claire's identical twin sister, Charlie."

Identical twin. Sister.

The words punch the air from my lungs.

"You didn't answer my question. How do you know Eli?" She annunciates every word, irritation seeping from her voice.

I run both hands over my face, like maybe I'll wake up from this mess if I scrub hard enough. "Shit." My voice comes out rough, too loud in the small diner booth.

"Well, this is a relief." I exhale, the tension draining from every muscle in my body. She's not a random girl, and this is all a misunderstanding. I'm *not* going to jail. My moment of celebration is short-lived when I feel her gaze burning a hole straight through me. Oh boy, she looks pissed. No amount of sugar and carbs will save me now. I need to start explaining the situation before she decides to bite my head off. I know too well the emotional roller coaster she's on right now. Her hormones are in the driver's seat, and I need to tread carefully.

I don't know what it is about her. She's a full foot shorter than me, but the look she's giving me tells me she will go full wrath-of-God on me if I don't start explaining soon.

Raising both hands, I face my palms out in surrender. "Look, before you bite my head off, I'm Eli's best friend and roommate, Aiden. He asked me to help with an immersive role-playing kidnapping scenario. Eli and Claire agreed on it prior to today. I was tasked with helping him kidnap her and taking her to the cabin on the outskirts of town that he rented for their, let's just say, excursion of the day. I unfortunately grabbed you instead of her, hence why we are in the current predicament." The words tumble out like I'm afraid that if I stop, she'll throw her hot cocoa at me and run away.

I let the silence fill the space so she can process everything that I just told her, praying that she believes me and doesn't think I'm a true kidnapper. It feels like an eternity before she finally speaks.

"How can I trust that you're Eli's best friend when you don't even know who his girlfriend is?"

"In my defense, I have not met her in person, and you guys are identical," I deadpan.

"That is no excuse." She eyes me skeptically.

"Look, if you don't trust me, just call your sister. I'm sure Eli is there with her and he can explain everything."

"How convenient, you're suggesting I reach out to my

sister when you took my phone from me." Her voice drips with sarcasm.

My mouth opens to speak, but I immediately close it, because she's got me there. I forgot I took her phone and put it in the glove compartment of the car.

"Well, why don't you use my phone and call Claire? Again, I'm sure Eli will be there to explain everything."

"Do you think I have people's phone numbers memorized? What is this, the 1990s?"

"Well, how do you suppose we go about the situation?"

Before she can respond, a deep, gravely male voice sounds from behind me. Instantly, I'm irritated that someone is interrupting our conversation.

"Charlie, is that you?"

Who is this guy, and why is he so chummy with her? I don't like it one bit. Judging from the face she's making, she's not a fan of him either.

"Hey, Kevin. How are you?" she asks.

"Good, good. Can't complain, the business is doing well, and Lisa's expecting our first child." His grin is smug, the kind that says he expects applause.

Something ticks in me—there's history here. The way Charlie's left eye twitches at the mention of Lisa, I'm starting to piece together that she isn't a fan of either of them.

"That's great to hear. I'm glad you guys are doing well." She gives a tight smile that doesn't quite reach her eyes.

"Yeah, I heard you moved back from the city. What happened? Did it get lonely out there by yourself?" His tone is dripping with condescension. It's enough to make me want to punch him right in his square face.

"Nothing like that. Just wanted to be closer to home while I get ready for my bakery opening. Maybe you heard of it, Charlie's Batter Co.?"

Judging from how big his eyes widen, he knows of her bakery.

"Oh, you're *that* Charlie?! Lisa loves your page. She's been wanting to order a cake for the baby shower, but it says you were close to taking custom orders?"

"Oh yes, I have a lot of interest, and I'm only taking a selected few clients right now." A wave of pride washes over me as she puts this guy in his place.

"Oh, well, for old time's sake, we would love it if you could fit us in." This guy has no shame. Seconds ago, he was trying to belittle her and now he wants a favor.

"Sure, why not? Have her send me an email, and I'll see what I can do." This girl is too nice for her own good.

"Thanks, well, I better grab the peach cobbler she sent me here for. That pregnancy craving is real." He looks at me and winks like we're best friends.

"Who is that?" I ask as soon as he's out of earshot.

"That," she says, slumping back down in her seat, all the energy she had draining from that interaction, "was my ex-boyfriend from high school. He dumped me a month before prom and then showed up at my house a week before prom, asking me to go with him." She resumes fidgeting with the sleeves of her sweater. "And now, I guess he is married to my archnemesis. Who he took to prom, by the way."

"Wow, what a couple."

"Yeah, I know, right. And the people pleaser in me just agreed to bake them something for their new bundle of joy." She chuckles, shaking her head.

"You could always tell them your oven broke down," I offer, hoping this new change of topic will help her trust me a bit.

"Ha! That's a good idea. I might take your advice on that." Her eyes lock with mine, and she gives me the first genuine smile I've seen since Kevin appeared.

"Now, back to our situation. How do you propose we situate," she gestures between the two of us, "this?"

"I promise you, I'm trustworthy. How about *I* pay, then we head to my car for your phone so you can call your sister." She hesitates for a moment, but I can see it in her eyes. She wants to trust me.

"All right, fine, we'll do it your way."

Chapter 19

Charlie

The gravel crunches underneath my shoes as we walk back to Aiden's car. Aiden. Eli's best friend. His roommate. The last few hours swirl in my head. It's not that I don't want to believe him; his explanation is very plausible. I know Claire's interest in books, and she has mentioned before that she has shared some fantasy with Eli. It's just hard to fully trust a complete stranger.

Aiden stops at his passenger side, looking sheepishly at me before opening the car door for me.

"See," he says, "a total gentleman."

I fight the grin that's trying to form on my face. Even though he gives off a scary bear vibe, he's really a teddy bear on the inside. Aiden gets in the driver's seat and glances over at me. He's being very gentle, like he's trying not to startle a wild animal.

"I'm just going to grab your phone from the glove compartment for you. Or I mean, you could do it if you're more comfortable."

"I can do it." I open the compartment and grab my phone. Only it's dead.

"It's dead. Do you have a charger?"

"Sure. Here."

Plugging my phone in, I stare out at the empty lot as we pull away from Maple Diner.

Silence fills the cabin. It's like now that our dynamic is no longer captor and captive, we have suddenly become two awkward people on a first date. Oh great, just like Dee Dee predicted.

"Well, I guess we can start heading back toward Main Street. Would you like me to drop you off at the bookstore?"

"Yes, that would be nice. Thank you."

"So, just to make sure we are on the same page. You won't call the sheriff on me as soon as we get back, right?"

"That depends."

"Depends on what?"

"How sorry you are for kidnapping me." The corner of my mouth twitches into a smirk.

"Super sorry. Scout's honor. Would I win any favor if you got to meet Jake today?"

"Oh, bribing me with your fur child, I see, that's an unfair advantage."

The ride back to Main Street is quicker than I want it to be. The storefronts blur by as we make our way down. The silence is awkward but comfortable.

"Do you and Eli work at the same hospital?" I ask, wanting to continue our previous easygoing conversation.

"Yeah, we're rotating at the same hospital right now and hope to get into their residency program."

I watch him from the corner of my eye, his hand resting loosely on the wheel, veins flexing with every turn. Gosh, I bet the nurses at the hospital love him. Those veins are probably their version of a jackpot.

"I bet the nurses love your forearms," I blurt before my brain can stop me. The words slip out way too casually, and the second they do, I want to reel them back in. *Way to have no filter, Charlie.*

He glances over, one brow raised. "My forearms?"

"Yeah, I donate blood once a quarter, and the nurses can never find my veins. My arm ends up looking like I went twelve rounds with a toddler holding a marker. Yours must be heaven to them." I'm oversharing again, but how else was I going to recover from complimenting his *veins*?

His nostrils flare, his jaw tightens, and I swear I see the muscles in his forearm flex tighter around the steering wheel.

"Where do you go?" he asks, his voice low, but there's something behind it I can't quite name.

"Where do I go?" I repeat dumbly, because my brain short-circuits at his tone.

"For blood draws."

"Oh. I usually drive in for the Brooksdale Medical Center quarterly blood drive."

He nods once, eyes still on the road. "Next time you give blood, come find me. I'll do it. That way you won't bruise."

I blink, caught off guard. My stomach does this weird swoopy thing at his protective tone. I stare at his face, unable to comprehend why he feels the need to draw my blood for me. His jaw ticks; he's focused, pretending not to notice me watching him, which makes me want to poke the bear.

"Sooooo," I say, dragging out the word and changing the topic so the butterfly in my stomach will stop fluttering at his odd version of protectiveness. "What are we?"

He chuckles, head tipping back against the seat. "You're kidding, right?"

I grin, unable to help it. "Oh, come on. You can't fake-kidnap someone, drive them around town, feed them, and then just drop them off like an Amazon return. There's gotta be some kind of label for us."

He glances my way, the corner of his mouth twitching. "Yeah. The label is: mistake I'll be paying for until I die."

"Harsh," I say, clutching my chest in mock offense, "and here I thought we had something special."

He exhales a quiet laugh under his breath that he tries to hide, but I catch it. And even though he doesn't say it, the look in his eyes says enough.

As we near The Lantern Nooks, I spot Claire waving frantically at a very apologetic-looking Eli. He's trying to calm her down while also juggling a puppy leash—attached to a fluffy little dog who looks two seconds away from bolting after a squirrel.

"Oh-em-gee, is that Jake?" I ask, my voice bubbling with excitement.

"Yeah, that's him." Aiden's lips twitch. "Looks like Eli's in damage control mode."

"Oh, you better brace yourself," I tease. "Claire takes self-defense classes. She's totally going to drop-kick you as soon as you're within range."

"I think I can manage." His eyes glance at Claire like he's trying to size her up.

The street parking is full, the festival likely in full swing, so we end up a few cars down from where we spot Claire and Eli. He executes that perfect three-point turn they teach you in driver's ed—one hand on the wheel, the other braced on the back of my seat—I had to check myself for any drool that results in the sight of his forearm flexing as he steers.

Making our way towards the arguing couple, I can tell my sister was two seconds from calling in the cavalry.

"God, where could she have gone?" Concern and panic are etched in Claire's voice.

"Do you think she stopped by the General Store to get more flour? Didn't you say she had an emergency order last night?" Eli's rubbing soothing circles up and down her arms.

"Maybe I should call Will, the sheriff; he could help us."

They're both too engrossed in their conversation to notice us approaching. Jake, however, doesn't miss a beat. He wiggles out of Eli's hold and comes barreling toward us, drawing both their attention. Claire's eyes lock with mine, and before I can even react, she's running toward me, arms wide, pulling me into a tight hug.

"Thank god you're okay!" she breathes out.

I hug her back tightly. "Yes, I'm okay. Just a little mistaken-identity trope in real life."

She pulls back, glaring. "What?"

Her gaze shifts past me, and when she spots Aiden, her eyes narrow. "Who are you?"

"This is Aiden. He's my roommate and best friend. I called him to help look for Charlie." Eli provides.

"But, you guys showed up together?" Claire looks between us, her brows furrow as she tries to piece together the situation.

Eli, seeming to realize that we did indeed walk up together, looked at Aiden in surprise. "Actually, yeah, why are you here together?"

"Should you tell them or should I?" I say, giving him a cheeky grin.

Aiden sighs, preparing himself to recount the most ridiculous fake-kidnapping scenario there ever was. "Look, I was just following your dumbass boyfriend's plan. He said you liked those dark romance books and convinced me to help kidnap you, but I accidentally napped your sister." Tossing his thumb in my direction as he finishes up his recount of the morning's event.

"What?!" Claire shouts in disbelief, looking at Eli, who is looking at her sheepishly.

"I did not know this." Eli lifts his hands in surrender. "Why didn't you tell me when I called earlier?"

"Well, earlier I didn't know she was Claire's sister. I thought I kidnapped a stranger."

"How could you not realize she wasn't the right girl?"

"They're identical!" Aiden shoots back. "You could've mentioned she had a twin sister!"

"I did mention she had a twin named Charlie!" Eli argues.

"Yeah, and I thought Charlie was a guy!"

Claire and I both burst out laughing at their married-couple bickering. The arguing duo stops at the sound of our laughter, as if suddenly remembering we're still here. I bend down to scratch Jake behind the ear before straightening to give Eli a quick side hug, then lift my gaze to meet Aiden's emerald green eyes.

"Okay, Mr. Grumpy Captor," I say through giggles. "Looks like our trope did turn from captors to lovers. How about we start over?"

Aiden chuckles. "Alright, princess, I'll play."

"Hi, my name's Charlotte, but everyone calls me Charlie." I wink at him.

Taking my hand and giving it a gentle squeeze, the gesture causes the butterflies in my stomach to flutter.

"Nice to meet you, Charlie. I'm Aiden. Would you maybe want to grab a cup of coffee with me sometime?"

I tilt my head, pretending to think. "That depends. Do you think you'll be able to spot me in a crowd this time?"

Chapter 20

Charlie

TWO YEARS LATER

I'm frantically running around my bakery to get everything set up. Today is the day! We're getting *engaged*! And by "we," I mean Claire, because obviously Eli gets us as a set.

Glancing around this beautiful space I curated, I can't help but let out a dreamy sigh. I did it! Charlie's Batter Co. is more than just a bakery—it's *my baby*. I opened the bakery a year ago and we instantly took off, quickly becoming part of the heartbeat on Main Street.

From the outside, it looks exactly how I imagined it the night I first sketched it out on a napkin—a French-inspired storefront with open glass doors and windows that let passersby see the freshly baked goods inside. Flower pots line the front of the store, creating a warm and inviting display.

The moment you walk in, you're wrapped in the warmth of vanilla, cinnamon, and freshly baked bread from the ovens. Directly to the left of the entrance are glass cases stacked with golden croissants, cream-filled pastries, and of course, my best sellers, the sourdough discard brownies. Multiple magazines have tried to get the recipe. Everyone wants to mimic the gooey, decadent, double-fudge brownies. Who knew sourdough discards could turn into a cult favorite? Doughbi-Wan, my faithful starter, was practically a silent partner in keeping this place alive. Marble bistro tables are scattered on the right, and each table is paired with bentwood chairs in soft cream, giving off the Parisian bakery vibe.

The bell above the bakery door chimes, and I glance up just in time to see Aiden walk in with a box tucked under one arm. My breath hitches the way it always does when he fills a doorway—broad shoulders, easy stride, that air of quiet confidence that makes it impossible to look away. I'll never get over how handsome he is. His jawline looks even sharper now that he's trimmed his beard shorter. He'd grumbled about "surgeon practicality" and how the shorter beard made it easier to get those beard covers on for the surgeries, but I wasn't complaining. Not one bit.

He landed a residency position at Brooksdale Medical Center, just like he wanted. It's still a two-hour drive from Everly Falls, but we make it work. Balancing a long-distance relationship and starting a business was tough, but Aiden never lets me forget how worth it we are. Every morning, without fail, I wake up to a text from him—sometimes hours after he's been on call, sometimes before the sun even rises. On the days he knows I'm running on fumes, lunch and dinner magically appear at my door. And when he realized I was skipping too many meals, he set up a weekly meal-prep subscription so I'd still have something warm and home-cooked waiting for me.

It's in the little things he does—the quiet thoughtfulness, the way he loves so completely, caring for others without ever asking for anything in return. Aiden isn't just a green flag—he's the whole damn field.

"Hi there, princess. You need help?" His familiar voice carries across the bakery, warm and a little weary. He's probably exhausted from driving after his shift. I make a mental note to whip up his favorite coffee of the season—white chocolate peppermint mocha. He's dressed in a pair of gray slacks and a blue polo with the sleeve rolled up to his elbow, his forearm on full display. Am I drooling? I swipe my thumb over the corner of my mouth to confirm. I'm good. For now.

"Yes, please!" I break into a full grin as he rounds the glass case. "Will you help me with the banner so I don't have to drag the step ladder out? You know how much I love exploiting our height difference."

His lips tug into the faintest smirk, and he shakes his head. "One of these days, you're going to climb that ladder and realize I've spoiled you rotten."

"Not today." I shove the rolled banner into his hands, making my way toward the vases of flowers I've haphazardly started arranging. "Besides, why risk my life when I have you?"

His eyebrows quirk in amusement. "Risk your life? It's a step stool, not Angel's Landing."

"Exactly," I toss back, missing our banter. "I'm not built for heights. I'm built for cakes."

He laughs, low and throaty, making the butterflies in my stomach take flight. He works so hard, and some days, his shift can take a mental toll. Any time I can make him laugh, it's like a small victory.

"Lila and Jade are on their way to help finish the setup, and Eli said he'd have Claire here by seven," I say, grabbing some rubber bands to secure the balloon garland for the fifth time. These garlands are harder to put together than those YouTube videos make them out to be. I severely underestimated the amount of time it would require, hence why I am still behind in setting up.

Glancing at the clock, I say over my shoulder, "Claire has

no idea he's popping the question tonight. I'm honestly shocked I haven't spoiled it already."

"You?" Aiden teases as he easily stretches to pin the banner where I'd been struggling. "Not being able to keep a secret? Shocking."

"Hey, in my defense, it's been torture. Especially when I suggested we go for a pampering session and get our nails done, she gave me the most suspicious side-eye, because she knows I *never* have polish. Too risky for the bakery."

He glances over his shoulder at me, eyes warm with amusement. "Let me guess, you caved and told her you just wanted 'sister bonding time?'"

I groan. "Exactly. And she bought it...I think. But I swear, the girl's going to sniff it out before Eli even pulls the ring out of his pocket."

Aiden finishes hanging the banner with ease, as we step back and admire his handiwork. Jade and Lila's voices drift in from the front door.

"He did not," Jade says.

"What didn't he do?" I ask, walking over to my best friends for a quick hug.

"Lila says her new beau set up a scavenger hunt for her in the airport while she had a layover between flights. He got all his coworkers in on it, and she basically spent the morning reliving the scene straight out of a Hallmark movie," Jade says, almost in disbelief.

"I know, it was so much fun. He's really sweet, and I'm so in over my head," she says dreamily.

Before I can press Lila more on her newest love interest, my phone buzzes with an incoming message from Ava.

AVA

Hi, I am running late! There was a deer standing in the middle of the road, and I didn't know what to do.

Luckily, this guy showed up and ushered
the deer off the road. It was kind of wild.

CHARLIE

Yeah, the wildlife here is definitely not
scared of us.

Do you know who helped you?

And no worries about being late. Eli said
he'll be here around 7pm. I'll leave the back
door open so you can come through the
back.

AVA

Perfect! You're amazing.

And I don't know, I tried to say "Thank you"
and get his name, but he just grunted at me
and got back in his truck.

He was pretty hot, in a grumpy kind of way,
but maybe that's my vagina talking. That
bitch is always thirsty over red flag men.

Stifling a laugh, I angle my body away from Aiden so he
doesn't question who I'm talking to. I don't think he would
appreciate talking about his sister's sexual needs.

CHARLIE

LOL, you're killing me. I'll introduce you to
some locals while you're in town.

Maybe a holiday distraction is what you
need to break out of your funk.

AVA

I'll hold you to it! I'll see you soon.

I pocket my phone and join my best friends in finishing up
the floral arrangement.

Ava and I quickly became friends after bonding over a dark mafia series we'd both been reading. She's kind, caring, and fiercely loyal to the people she loves—and I'm lucky she considers me one of them. Even if Aiden and I go our separate ways one day, I know Ava and I will always be friends.

At a quarter till six, all our friends and families start trickling in. First, my grandparents, parents, followed by Eli's parents, then Dee Dee and Pop, and their son, Everett.

"They're walking down Main Street." Aiden's voice rises over the chatter of excitement.

Walking over to Aiden's side, I spot Ava hustling through the back hallway before abruptly stopping. I follow her line of sight and land on Everett—interesting.

I turn back to Aiden, sliding my arm around his, excitement bubbling over. I'm grinning ear to ear, still in disbelief that a fake kidnapping led me to him.

Turns out, I didn't just get tied up that morning.

I got tied up for love.

Epilogue

Aiden

I blink awake to sunlight spilling across soft sheets and the faint whiff of cinnamon rolls drifting in from the kitchen. My stomach grumbles to life. Charlie must be up early, testing another new recipe. Of course she is. Six months after opening her bakery in the heart of Main Street, she's already been featured in more magazines than I can count.

I still can't believe our little "mishap" led me to her. She's the piece I didn't know I was missing—steady, grounding, endlessly understanding about my long shifts and late nights. Always checking in, reminding me to eat, to breathe, and to rest. I make it a point to visit her and Everly Falls as often as I can. I even started looking into clinic openings here for when I finish my program. She's thriving here, and this town, it's beginning to feel like home for us.

I glance around her cozy bedroom, sunlight slanting across the picture of Charlie, Jake, and I at her grand opening. She's smiling ear to ear as she cuts the ribbon. I couldn't be prouder, and I'm grateful to have this weekend off from my residency to soak up some time with her.

I whistle for my little furball, Jake, but I hear no sign of him in the apartment. Typical. You'd think Charlie was the one who adopted him, considering he only comes to me when he needs something—a potty break, treats, or belly rubs. I'm pretty much the spare human to him. It doesn't help that Mrs. Bennett spoils him every time he's in town. She always has a fresh bag of treats or another ridiculous seasonal outfit. Honestly, he's got a better wardrobe than I do.

The door creaks open and Charlie steps in, cheeks flushed from the morning chill. Jake's tucked in her arm like a football. "Morning," she says softly, brushing a few strands of hair from her face. "We took a walk before breakfast."

I sit up, smiling as I motion her closer. She puts Jake down, and he scurries into the kitchen. Five dollars says she left him a peanut butter-filled Kong toy there. When she settles beside me, I pull her into my arms, right where she belongs. I squeeze her tight, inhaling her sweet vanilla scent. "Good morning, princess. How was your walk?"

"It was nice. We ran into Mrs. Whittaker. She said her grandson's moving back to town."

"He's the one that hasn't been back in a while, right?"

"Yep, almost six years now," she says with a grin. "He was Jade's high school sweetheart. They didn't end on good terms. If you're okay with sharing me for a few hours, I want to check in with her after breakfast before our weekend festivities."

I chuckle, nuzzling into her neck. "You know I would never share you willingly but I know how important this is to you. Jake and I will head to the dog park while we wait."

She hums, tilting her head slightly, letting my lips brush the edge of her jaw. "Someone has been working on his bedside manner."

I laugh softly. "Only for you."

She slips out of my hold, brushing her fingers across my

chest as she stands. "Alright, sleeping beauty, get up. Your cinnamon roll's warming in the oven."

"Is this the new recipe you were talking about?"

Her eyes light up. "Yes, the Ube cinnamon roll. It's going on the seasonal menu if it passes your taste test."

I inhale deeply, catching the scent of butter, sugar, and that hint of sweet purple yam. "You're dangerous, you know that?"

Charlie laughs, nudging my leg with her knee. "You keep saying that."

"Because it's true," I murmur, tugging her gently back toward me. "Between the baked goods and the way you're looking at me right now—I'm doomed."

She tries to look unimpressed, but her smile gives her away. "Maybe a little doom isn't so bad."

I grin, standing up and pulling her back into my embrace. "Depends on how sweet the ending is."

Her breath catches, and before she can respond, I close the distance between us, kissing her slow and easy. She tastes like whipped cream, coffee, and everything good about mornings.

When she finally pulls back, her voice is soft, teasing. "You still want that cinnamon roll?"

"Later," I murmur against her lips, already tugging her back closer.

Jake barks from the kitchen, breaking the spell, and we laugh.

"Come on," she says, pushing at my chest. "Jake waits for no one."

I watch her walk away, sunlight catching the edges of her hair, and I know for certain, this life is perfect.

Review

Did you enjoy Tied Up for Love?
Please consider leaving a review on your favorite platform.

Want to read more about Aiden and Charlie?
Scan the QR code or click here for the bonus epilogue.

Warning: **This bonus epilogue contains sexually explicit scenes and language. Please read with care.**

Acknowledgments

I still can't believe this book is out in the world. This story has been living rent-free in my head for so long, and it wasn't until the gentle push from my two book besties and my husband's unwavering support of my delulu dreams.

To Brittany and Kelsey, special thank yous for your endless encouragement and believing in this story.

To my husband, thank you for always cheering on my never-ending stream of new ideas.

All the hugs and forehead kisses to my honorary advisor, Grace Pearce. It was a job you didn't ask for, but I appreciate you for answering all my questions. Grace is the author of *Leigh Makes Three*, *The Ex List*, *Perfect Praise*, *Xantera*, and *Veradel*. If you have not read her books, I highly encourage you to check them out.

Thank you, Cassidy, for your editing support and Sara, for final proof reading.

To my alpha and beta readers, your feedback shaped this story into what it is today, and I am so thankful you were along on this journey.

And lastly, thank you to you, the readers who took a chance on this indie author.

About the Author

Writing under a pen name, Nora Lane is a Vietnamese romance writer, a mom, a wife, a pharmacist, and a coffee addict. She lives in Oklahoma, with her husband and two boys, but wishes to one day be in a state that doesn't experience all four seasons in one day.

Living in her own grumpy x sunshine, friends-to-lovers, workplace romance happily-ever-after, she writes short, sweet, and fun stories for readers who need a quick escape.

To stay up to date with upcoming releases, join Nora Lane's Newsletter:
https://noralanewrites.myflodesk.com/newsletter

instagram.com/noralanewrites
tiktok.com/@noralanewrites
threads.com/noralanewrites

Also by Nora Lane

Love, Delivered

Sara Mei Lin is perfectly content living life indoors—streaming League of Legends to thousands of viewers, surviving on late-night deliveries, and keeping her heart safely guarded after a devastating betrayal. The outside world is optional. DoorDash is not.

What Sara doesn't know is that her preferred Dasher, Dave, is the neighbor she's been crushing on.

Dave Francis Rosenberg signs up to be a Dasher as a distraction from the pressure of respiratory therapy school—not to catch feelings. But when one customer's orders come with witty banter and an unexpected spark, Dave finds himself looking forward to every notification.

As messages turn flirtatious and boundaries blur, Dave must decide if he's brave enough to step out from behind the screen and confess the secret he's been hiding—or if his self-doubt will cause him to lose the girl he's been yearning for.

Grab you signed copies from: https://noralaneauthor.com/